"On the count of five, be ready to cover me!"

"One, two, three, four . . ." Kincaid's voice sounded hollow in his ears, and his body tensed while incoming rounds continued to slam into the rocks and sing their dying, screeching song. "Five!"

The three Springfields fired simultaneously and were quickly followed by a volley from the second three, while the first group reloaded.

Kincaid sprinted forward and stooped over Pappas, the sweat dripping from his forehead and onto the wounded man's shirt as he rolled him onto his back. One shot, lucky or aimed, tore through the left shoulder of Kincaid's tunic, ripping cloth and bringing an instant flood of crimson to the surface. Matt could feel the searing burn across his upper shoulder, but he ignored the pain and backed toward the outcropping, dragging Pappas behind him.

"Hang on, Private," Matt grunted. "I'll either get you out of their sights or we'll be dead together . . ."

EASY COMPANY

EASY COMPANY AND THE GREEN ARROWS

JOHN WESLEY HOWARD

A JOVE BOOK

First Jove edition published April 1981

First printing

Printed in the United States of America

Jove books are published by Jove Publications, Inc., 200 Madison Avenue, New York, NY 10016

Also in the Easy Company series from Jove

EASY COMPANY AND THE SUICIDE BOYS
EASY COMPANY AND THE MEDICINE GUN

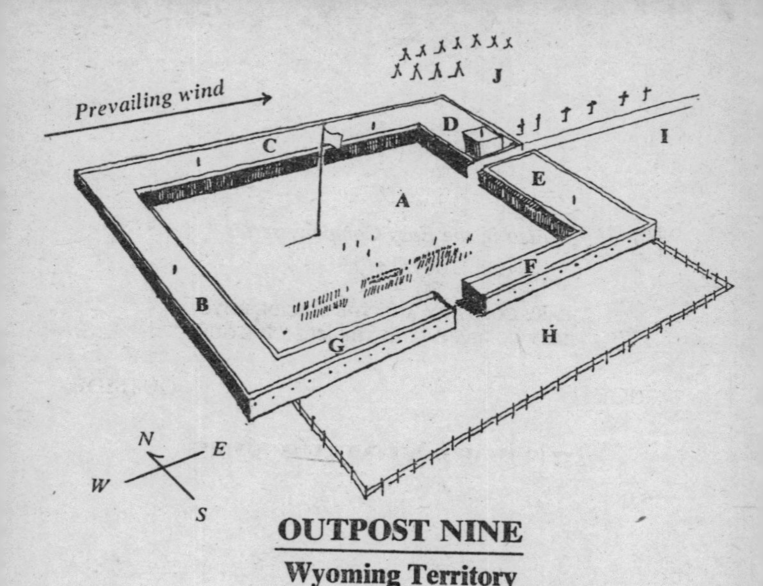

OUTPOST NINE

Wyoming Territory

KEY

A. Parade and flagstaff

B. Officers' quarters ("officers' country")

C. Enlisted men's quarters: barracks, day room, and mess

D. Kitchen, quartermaster supplies, ordnance shop, guardhouse

E. Suttler's store and other shops, tack room, and smithy

F. Stables

G. Quarters for dependents and guests; communal kitchen

H. Paddock

I. Road and telegraph line to regimental headquarters

J. Indian camp occupied by transient "friendlies"

INTERIOR OUTSIDE

OUTPOST NUMBER NINE
(DETAIL)

Outpost Number Nine is a typical High Plains military outpost of the days following the Battle of the Little Big Horn, and is the home of Easy Company. It is not a "fort"; an official fort is the headquarters of a regiment. However, it resembles a fort in its construction.

The birdseye view shows the general layout and orientation of Outpost Number Nine; features are explained in the Key.

The detail shows a cross-section through the outpost's double walls, which ingeniously combine the functions of fortification and shelter.

The walls are constructed of sod, dug from the prairie on which Outpost Number Nine stands, and are sturdy enough to withstand an assault by anything less than artillery. The roof is of log beams covered by planking, tarpaper, and a top layer of sod. It also provides a parapet from which the outpost's defenders can fire down on an attacking force.

one

First Lieutenant Matt Kincaid stood atop the eastern wall of Outpost Number Nine and felt the first gentle kiss of the rising sun brush across his tanned, handsome face. Although there was yet a coolness lingering from the night's chill, he knew the day would turn warm, then hot with something nearing a sudden vengeance. But as he stood there, tall, muscular and every inch a military man in both posture and demeanor, the faded blue of his forage dress uniform contrasting with the dull brown of the cut-sod wall, his mind was not on the heat of the coming day. His eyes and his thoughts were locked on two mounted men, both wearing buckskins with fringed trimming and holding elbow-cradled rifles in constant readiness, who were nearing the outpost from the direction of the tipi ring several hundred yards toward the northeast.

Behind and below him, Kincaid could hear the sounds of a military unit coming to life. The men of Easy Company moved to their assigned details and morning chores with no more than the normal amount of grumbling and complaining about the vicissitudes of army life. They had long ago accepted the fact that outpost duty was, by nature, an admixture of boredom and the ultimate thrill of facing death in battle. As part of a mounted infantry regiment, Easy Company had been assigned the sometimes precarious task of guarding the vital communications link between the Little Big Horn and the South Pass over the Rockies, as well as maintaining a strong American military presence in the heart of Indian country.

Recognizing the rider to the right, Lieutenant Kincaid smiled and studied his chief scout, Windy Mandalian. Windy was easily the most independent yet reliable, deadly yet compassionate, total man of the Plains he had ever known. There was about Mandalian a certain uncanny ability to perceive the thinking of the red man in a manner that made him seem equally as much Indian as he was white. There was a prominent hook to his nose, and because of his dark features, high cheekbones, and narrow face, he was often mistaken by white travelers passing through the area for a Cheyenne, and to Matt's knowledge, Windy Mandalian had never once denied it or offered correction.

Kincaid had never seen Mandalian's companion before, and now, as the two riders were lost to his view when they entered the outpost, Kincaid turned away from the wall and descended the steps onto the packed earth of the parade. Mandalian turned his horse in Matt's direction and the second rider followed. They met by the flagstaff in the center of the square, and Mandalian pulled his horse in before leaning back with a comfortable slouch in his saddle.

"Mornin', Matt," Windy offered, chewing laconically on a cheekful of cut-plug.

"Good morning, Windy," Kincaid replied, while the slight smile returned again to his face. "Up and stirring about a little early this morning, aren't you?"

"Depends on what you're comparing it to," Windy said, nodding toward his companion. "Lieutenant Kincaid, meet Seth Daniels. Me and Seth trapped beaver together up in the Milk River country a few winters back. His word's as good as his shootin' eye, which, if I remember right enough, ain't been bested by many men."

Kincaid stepped forward and offered his hand, which the trapper leaned down to receive with power and enthusiasm.

"Pleased to meet you, Mr. Daniels," Matt said cordially, "and welcome to Outpost Nine. Whatever we have is at your disposal. Please make yourself comfortable. A friend of Windy's is a friend of ours."

Daniels smiled his appreciation as he said, "Thank you, Lieutenant. I won't be havin' much time to stay, but a cup of coffee sounds mighty good, then maybe we should talk, which is why I come by this way in the first place." Daniels grinned openly. "That and to see how ugly the squaws are that this old bastard is sleepin' with nowadays."

"And?" Windy asked with a mocking stare.

"Ugly. Downright sinful ugly."

"Seth, you don't know ugly from a horse's ass. Now let's go get that coffee and you can tell the lieutenant what you've got to say and not keep an important man waiting."

Daniels clapped Windy across the back with a hearty laugh, which Windy returned in equal measure as they stepped from their mounts and followed Kincaid to the officer's mess.

When they were seated with their coffee, the trapper asked, "Why don't you tell the lieutenant what I told you, Windy? I'll fill in whatever you leave out or what I forgot in the first place."

Mandalian nodded, then sipped his coffee as his eyes went to Kincaid's face. "Seth just came down from the north, through Arapaho country, and he says word got to him that some medicine man up there—what was his name, Seth? Gray Bear?"

Daniels nodded over the cup moving to his lips. "Yup. Gray Bear. Who the hell ever saw a gray bear?"

"I'm familiar with Gray Bear," Kincaid said. "He was a signatory to the treaty which put the Arapaho back on their ancestral hunting ground, and to my knowledge, he's a man of honor and integrity."

Windy frowned. "Let's hope so, Matt, but that ain't quite the way Seth heard it. Accordin' to what he heard from some stockmen in the area, this Gray Bear might be trying to stir his people up and maybe get 'em back on the warpath. They say he's been promising his tribe 'new green arrows, as far as the eye can see. Arrows from Great Turtle, who wants us to live in the ways of the Grandfather Times.' Now, I'm sure you're the last man who needs remindin' that the Arapaho paint green stripes on their war arrows and that the 'Grandfather Times' means before the white man took their land away."

Matt Kincaid swirled the coffee remaining in his cup and shook his head. "I can't understand it. The Arapaho have just settled down after the Custer fight, they were given back their old hunting grounds for that purpose, and the man from the Bureau of Indian Affairs assigned to them is fair and doing the best he can for them. Gray Bear knows that any Indian leader who reneges on the treaties can and will be arrested and very likely executed. He is an old man. Why would he like to see more of his people die in a futile resumption of a war he cannot possibly win?"

"Beats me, Matt," Windy said, stretching his long legs beneath the table and hooking his hands behind his head. "But remember, if they rise again they will be on familiar ground in the foothills where they love to fight. And that reserve of theirs is pretty damned close to the approaches to the South Pass and both the rail and telegraph lines. Could be a real ballbuster if they decide to paint up again."

Kincaid turned to the trapper. "What do you make of it, Mr. Daniels? Did they seem about to go on the warpath when you were up there?"

"Well, as you might guess, Lieutenant, I make a pretty serious effort to stay away from as many Indians as I can on the open plains. Helps keep the hairline in one place. The only thing I'm tellin' you, or know for that matter, is what those stockmen told me. They seem to think the Arapaho are goin' to try and run them off their grazing land, which borders on the Arapaho reserve, and I can tell you for a fact that they are willin' to fight, if not spoilin' for one."

Matt sighed wearily. "So we've got the stockmen on one side, the Arapaho on the other, the Bureau of Indian Affairs in the middle, and nobody knowing for sure what the other person is talking about. I guess I'd better meet with Captain Conway and see if he wants us to take a patrol up there and check things out." He rose and extended his hand to the trapper. "Thank you for your concern and taking the time to come out of your way to inform us of this possible problem. I'll send a soldier to feed and water your horse and refit you with whatever provisions you might need. If you would care for breakfast, just tell the cook and you will be taken care of. Windy? I'd like to talk with you after I've seen the captain."

"I'll be around."

"Good. I think we will be riding north this morning."

Lieutenant Kincaid stepped from the mess and angled toward the orderly room. He glanced toward the sun and estimated the time to be nearly eight o'clock. As he stepped into the front office, he saw the first sergeant, Acting Master Sergeant Ben Cohen, already at his desk. Kincaid closed the door and Sergeant Cohen looked up from the duty roster spread before him. He was approximately forty years of age, big, beefy, and thick through the shoulders and chest. His hands were gnarled stumps with blunt fingers protruding; the evidence of much 'behind the barracks' discipline was revealed through scars, and twisted joints and knuckles.

"Good morning, sir," Cohen said, smiling easily with the gap between his front teeth showing as a narrow black line. "I guess when my shitlist gets longer than my regular list, I won't have any problem assigning details, will I?"

"Morning, Sergeant," Matt returned with a chuckle. "Who's the newest addition?"

"Private Radcliff. Guess he didn't salute Lieutenant Davis fast enough to please the good sir."

"Radcliff? First Platoon, Second Squad?"

"Yes sir."

"The First is Davis' platoon, isn't it?"

"Yes sir. It has been for nearly two days now. Ever since he arrived here in a cloud of dust and ridiculous assumptions about Indian fighting."

"Well, don't worry about finding any particularly nasty little jobs for Radcliff. I think he'll be going on patrol with me this morning, along with Lieutenant Davis, and maybe they both might learn something from the experience. Is Captain Conway in?"

"Yes sir," Cohen responded, rising and moving toward the door to the commanding officer's office. "Excuse me, sir. Lieutenant Kincaid to see you."

"Send him in, Sarge."

"Thanks," Matt said, stepping around the sergeant. "Be prepared to have the First Platoon ready to move out within the hour, rationed and equipped for several days in the field."

"Yes sir."

Matt stepped into the captain's office, and the CO looked up from the dispatch he was drafting to regimental headquarters. "Good morning, Matt. Have a seat there and let me just finish this damned little note asking why it is impossible for the men of this command to get paid on time. As you know, I write one of these per month, so I've pretty well got it down."

Matt eased into a chair before the captain's desk and watched silently while the older man finished his letter. Somewhere in his mid-forties, graying at the temples but still commanding a lean and hard physique, the captain should have been a major, particularly in light of the fact that he had served as a lieutenant colonel during the War, but he had been passed over again by the promotions board. He looked every bit the Virginian that he was, but as regular army he had fought for the North in the Union Army under General Grant. No matter what personal disappointments he had suffered, however, Captain Conway retained his Southern pride and dignity, and was army to the marrow of his bones.

"What can I do for you this morning, Matt?" Conway asked while he creased his letter into three folds and stuffed it into an envelope. The captain was not given to small talk, and he watched his adjutant closely as he sealed the envelope.

Kincaid shifted his long, lean frame in the chair and adjusted the hat perched upon a crossed knee. "Well, sir, we either have an Arapaho uprising on our hands, or just a bunch of people getting nervous over nothing. I'm not sure just which it is."

"Explain."

Matt told of his conversation with Seth Daniels, then said, "The Arapaho are damned difficult to understand, both in language and actions. Although he didn't come right out and say it, sir, I'm convinced that Windy thinks we should check this out. I'm afraid I agree with him."

Conway was silent for several moments before saying, "Yes, I don't think this is something we can just ignore. I can't understand Gray Bear calling for any uprising, though, and I'm not certain I believe it. He was against the Arapaho joining the Dakota Confederacy under Red Cloud in the first place, and he knows that any violation of the treaty he signed could be a hanging offense, with his own neck in the noose. I think you'd better take a platoon and head on up there. I heard you tell Sergeant Cohen to make First Platoon ready for patrol. Any particular reason you chose that platoon?"

"Yes," Matt answered without hesitation. "I think Lieutenant Davis might well profit through tempering of all that textbook knowledge he has with a little practical experience in the field. And there are some things I would like to learn about Private Radcliff. He's got the makings of a good soldier, but his attitude is definitely shit-house."

"I agree, for what little I know of either of them. Have a good, safe patrol, Matt. Use your best judgment and I'll back you one hundred percent on the outcome."

"Thank you, sir," Matt responded, moving toward the door. "We shouldn't be gone more than a week."

"However long it takes, do the job right. And Matt?" Kincaid stopped and turned, framed in the doorway.

"Yes, sir?"

"You know how I feel about these Indians, whether Arapaho, Sioux, or Cheyenne. They are to be treated firmly but fairly. Don't look for trouble, but if anyone has a lesson coming, make it a good one. The ink is still wet on those treaties we signed, and I don't think now would be a prudent time to demonstrate any weakness."

"I understand, sir, and agree completely." He paused and the two men looked at each other. "Tell me, Captain, just what in the hell are we doing, letting cattlemen graze their stock right up to the boundaries of the Arapaho reservation? That's kind of like locking a dog and a cat in the same closet, isn't it?"

Conway nodded in agreement. "You're right, Matt, it is. But we aren't the ones letting them, the Department of the Interior is. Over my objections, and those of everyone else who knows his ass from a teakettle, they issued those grazing permits with no limitations other than the boundaries established in the treaty. I don't think many of those longhorns read the damned thing and they're bound to wander across from time to time. Check the permits of any ranchers you encounter, and make sure their papers are legal and up to date. That's about all we can do."

"And if they aren't?"

"Then tell them to legalize or move out."

"Fine, sir," Kincaid said, adjusting his campaign hat on his head. "See you when we get back."

"Have a good patrol, and be careful. I need your help around here."

"I will, sir. I just hope this thing isn't as big as it sounds like it could be."

"Me too, Matt. Let's try to put a lid on it before it gets out of hand."

"I'll do my best, sir," Kincaid said as he stepped out the door.

two

The Rockies loomed high and majestic to the north. Their upper reaches were yet capped with snow, and the sparkling white outlined against the deep blue sky seemed symbolic of purity and peace within the Brotherhood of Man. And the verdant foothills, rolling in a sea of grass that caressed the earth with gentle strokes on a lilting breeze, stretched before the platoon of mounted infantry working its way northward, with Matt Kincaid and Windy Mandalian at the head of a column of twos.

"Probably the most beautiful country in the world, wouldn't you say, Windy?" Matt asked, drawing in a deep breath and exhaling the pure air scented by the scattered groves of conifers they were now passing through.

"Yup," Windy grunted. "And the most unforgiving."

"I'm a little surprised to see the grass so plentiful at this elevation."

"Don't be, Matt. All we've seen is a few scattered herds of pronghorn and elk, not to mention some sign but no trace of buffalo. When there ain't nothin' left to eat the grass, it should do pretty well."

They were nearing the crest of a swale nestled in the foothills, and Windy heard it first, then Matt. The officer raised his hand sharply and the column came to a halt while the scout slipped from his horse and ran in a low crouch off to one side. The muffled pounding of hooves in the tall grass became clearer, possibly three horses maybe four, followed by a distant rumble of several more horses. Before Matt could respond and form his platoon into a defensive unit, three straining ponies broke from a stand of timber, hooves driving at full speed and mouths twisted against woven-hair hackamores. Upon their backs were three young braves, crouched low against their horses' withers and molded as one with their animals. The green warpaint on their faces and encircling their upper arms and chests created an eerie deadliness about them which belied their youth. Intent upon their escape, the Indians were unaware of the platoon of soldiers cresting the ridge, even though they hesitated as they cleared the trees.

Their horses broke stride for no more than an instant before the lead brave wheeled his mount and plunged into the ravine, followed by the other two. Clumps of sod and grass flew from their horses' hooves.

Matt Kincaid held the pistol in his hand high above his head, as indication for the men behind him to hold their fire. Seasoned veterans that they were, they watched the retreating Indian mounts in silence and contained the desire for action.

Matt looked across at where Windy had taken up a position, some seventy-five yards away and crouched with his rifle resting against the trunk of a huge fir tree. He acknowledged the scout's nod toward the sound of the pursuing horses.

"Lieutenant Kincaid?" an excited voice said from behind him. "Second Lieutenant Davis requests permission to take a squad of troopers and establish pursuit of the green-faced heathen."

Matt could not conceal the look of contempt crossing his face, and his words came out more sharply than expected. "Permission denied, Lieutenant! Now get back there and make certain your platoon is properly deployed in defendable positions."

"Yes *sir*!" Davis snapped, the sound of his voice irritating Matt before the young lieutenant faded from his mind and his thoughts returned to the horses thundering toward them. He glanced once toward the platoon. Each man was lying prone on the lee side of the gentle ridge, Springfields aimed toward the opening in the trees while their mounts were held in the bottom of the swale by handlers. Davis moved upright among the troops, and Kincaid silently damned him. Then the first horse burst through the trees, a beautiful, rangy, foam-flecked roan with nostrils flared and neck arched against the reins. The rider, seated on a silver studded saddle of the finest tooled leather, was leaning forward, intent on the hoofprints in the grass and oblivious to the soldiers above him. He was young, lean, and tall, and as he leaned forward, hunched close to the roan's neck, Matt noticed a handsome wildness about him.

The shot was like a crack of lightning, rolling across the draw on echoing thunder. The roan pitched forward, dead before it fell, and the cattleman catapulted over its neck to land in a sprawled heap, ten yards in front of where the horse fell in a forward somersault. The other riders behind him, now breaking into the opening, wheeled their rearing, plunging mounts and raced back to the safety of the thicket. The rider who had been thrown scrambled on hands and knees, pulling the pistol from his holster as he moved, and tumbled into a cut bank, firing a shot as he disappeared, which snapped over the heads of the troops along the ridge. A volley of shots came from the thicket, and Matt heard Davis give the order to fire. The Springfields exploded on command and a hail of lead ripped into the stand of timber.

Matt Kincaid was dumbfounded for a second. In an instant he realized that the young Arapaho braves, unaware of the presence of the army unit, had set up an ambush for the pursuing cattlemen, and, in their haste to count coup, had fired upon their pursuers too early. And with the shot fired by the fallen cattleman, Lieutenant Davis had given the order to return fire. Now two friendlies were engaged in a fierce firefight while the instigators made a leisurely withdrawal.

"Hold your fire, men, goddammit! Hold your fire!" Matt bellowed over the roar of muzzle blasts. "Davis! You bring that platoon under control or I'll have your ass for breakfast!"

Fire from the ridge ceased immediately, but the cattlemen below continued their steady barrage. "Hold your fire down there!" Matt raged again. "We're United States Army, Easy Company, First Platoon, Mounted Infantry!"

Matt heard a voice rise from behind the cutbank. "Hold your fire, Ernie! Tell the boys to be ready, but wait for my signal!" The voice turned toward the ridge. "Hey, you up there, soldier boy! Show yourself and I'll do the same!"

Matt stood from where he lay in the tall grass and stepped to the lip of the ridge. "Lieutenant Davis? Have your men keep their weapons at the ready, but no one is to fire unless I am fired upon or until I give the command. Is that understood?"

"Yessir."

Matt heard Davis instructing his platoon as he moved down the hill, but his interest was given to the young cattleman rising from behind the cut bank. He knew Windy Mandalian's Sharps was trained on the man's chest at that precise moment, and any sign of treachery would bring instant death. Matt judged the man to be around twenty-two years of age, and the long blond hair curling about his face in a careless tousle made him seem equally as pretty as he was handsome.

Ignoring Kincaid, the young rider retrieved his hat from the ground, dusted it against his leg, then knelt beside his horse for a moment before rising to face the tall, square-shouldered man in blue.

"You killed my best horse," he said, his tone flat and accusing.

"Sorry, friend. I didn't, nor did my men. The death of that horse saved your life."

The contempt in the cattleman's voice was matched by the curling sneer on his lips. "What do you mean by that, soldier boy? And besides, what are you doing, ambushing American citizens? I thought you were sent here to protect taxpaying settlers like myself, instead of trying to kill them."

Struggling to control the heat rising in his chest, Matt said in a low, clear voice, "You are not talking to a 'soldier boy.' You are addressing First Lieutenant Matthew Kincaid, United States Army. You would do well to remember that, and to get your facts straight. Your horse was shot out from under you by the people you were trying to catch. If you *had* caught them, you would be dead now. You weren't ambushed. After you fired toward the ridge where my troops were positioned, one of my officers exercised poor judgment, for which I apologize, and ordered return fire. And, lastly, I am here to *protect* settlers like yourself, but we will need some help from you to accomplish that goal. Like not grazing your cattle on ground set aside by the Bureau of Indian Affairs as part of the rightful Arapaho reserve."

"I'm not grazing my cattle on their fucking land! I have a grazing permit from the Department of the Interior and Land Management, authorizing me to graze up to their boundaries."

"I would like to see those permits."

"Sure, but you'll have to come to the main ranch. My sister keeps them in a safe."

"Fine, we'll do that," Matt said, detecting a thaw in the young cattleman's hostile attitude. "Why were you in pursuit of those three braves, if I may ask?"

"Sure, you can ask. They killed a beef of mine and were draggin' it away when we caught 'em."

Matt watched the other man closely. "As I said, my name is Lieutenant Kincaid. What is yours?"

"Ramsey. David Ramsey."

"Mr. Ramsey," Matt said, nodding his head and waiting for an offered hand, which never came. He smiled easily and continued, "Let me ask you, Mr. Ramsey, how many cattle have you got on this particular stretch of range?"

"Around a thousand head. Why?"

"And of that thousand head being grazed so close to reservation ground, wouldn't it be difficult for you to make certain that none of your stock strayed across the boundary?"

Ramsey hesitated momentarily, locking eyes with Matt, then glancing away. "Yeah, it's tough."

"I figured as much. On which side of the boundary was your animal slain?"

"Can't tell for sure. Could have been shot on our side and drug across to theirs."

"Shall we see? Surely, in this deep grass, a trail would be left. I have a civilian scout with me who could determine instantly the circumstances."

"Aw, to hell with it," Ramsey said, stooping to remove the tack from the dead horse. "I don't give a shit whose side it was on. We'd seen where some other stock had crossed. Went over to get 'em and jumped them three feather-heads butchering another one. Pissed me off, so I went after 'em. No big deal. We'll square accounts later."

Matt signaled for Davis to assemble the platoon before speaking to Ramsey again. "You're wrong, I'm afraid, Mr. Ramsey. It *is* a big deal. Did you get a good look at those braves?"

"Mostly back and ass," Ramsey returned with a grunt as he dragged the cinch strap from beneath the horse.

"They were wearing warpaint, my friend," Matt said softly. "To me, that makes it a *very* big deal."

three

With the cattle hands riding ahead of them in an undisciplined cluster, the men of Easy Company followed in a precise column of twos on a course set for the main buildings of the Bucking R cattle spread. As they moved through the tranquil, almost parklike rangeland now becoming increasingly populated with longhorns, Kincaid thought about Lieutenant Davis and wondered if a second lieutenant's bars were something that could be had in the army of the day simply for their purchase price. Shaking Davis from his mind, Matt turned toward Windy, riding by his side.

"That was quite a skirmish back there, huh, Windy? Lucky no one was hurt."

The scout squinted toward a distant ridge and spat a stream of brown tobacco juice, which smacked against a boulder partially obscured in the grass. "Yeah, lucky, Matt. But not surprisin'. Ain't nobody could see nobody to shoot at anyways. Waste of ammunition." Then he added, almost as an afterthought, "That feller of yours is gonna need a little less schoolhousin' and a little more roughhousin' if he's gonna make it out here."

"I'm aware of that, Windy. He'll either have to prove himself or be cashiered, one or the other. I plan to have a man-to-man with him the first chance I get, but that's something that can't be done in front of the troops. What do you make of those three young bucks with their paint and all? Think there might be some truth to that story Seth told us about an uprising?"

Mandalian worked the chaw in his cheek, then shifted it to the other side. "They had on war grease, right enough. Could be just a few youngsters trying to gain a reputation. Then again, they might be part of an honest-to-Christ war party." Windy spat again, this time with a hint of contempt. "Could be they just got a little tired of Ramsey's cattle grazing on their land."

Matt nodded his agreement. "I can understand that. But I

can't understand, nor accept, the warpaint. That is in direct violation of the treaty. If the Arapaho wish to be treated fairly and given equal justice under the law, which I, and Captain Conway, intend to see that they receive, it's imperative that they abide by the terms of the treaty to the letter."

"And Ramsey?" Windy asked, shifting his rifle to a more comfortable position in the crook of his arm. "What do you think he would do if he found some Arapaho ponies grazing on his side of the boundary? Say, 'Shoo, little horsies, go home now'? Fuck no, he wouldn't. They would be dead, and Ramsey didn't sign no treaties, so he can't break none."

"That's true, no doubt, but he is still bound by the law."

"The white man has no law to bind him up here, Matt. Only the Indian is bound by the law, which he can't rightly understand, fathom, or comprehend. The things that once made him a man now make him a criminal. Kind of a piss-poor trade-off, I'd say."

Kincaid looked across and grinned. "You know, Windy, the one thing that irritates me about you is your goddamned frontier logic. You're right too damned much of the time." Then his face turned serious and his attention went to the corrals and the low, silhouetted log houses now materializing in the distance. "Good, bad, or indifferent, it's the only system we've got, Windy," he said softly. "Until somebody comes up with something better, we've got to try to make this one work. That must be the Ramsey outfit up ahead. Don't seem to be doing too bad for themselves."

Windy's eyes were on the buildings, situated on the open prairie, well away from the stand of timber to the rear, and facing to the south in deference to the prevailing north wind. "Yup. Whoever built it knew what they were doin'. Picked the best damned piece of ground the Arapaho ever had."

The cowhands were stepping down from their mounts in front of the cookshack, and Dave Ramsey, riding double behind the ramrod named Ernie, slid off the short, stocky man's mount and approached the army detachment waiting respectfully a short distance away. He was limping slightly, his left leg having stiffened from an injury suffered in the fall, when he approached Kincaid's horse.

"What was your name again?" he asked with indifference in his voice.

"Kincaid," Matt replied. "Lieutenant Matt Kincaid. This is Windy Mandalian, chief scout for Easy Company."

Ramsey glanced toward Windy with something of a superior expression on his face, which prompted another stream of spittle to course from the scout's lips and splash dangerously close to the young cattleman's boots. With a slight grin touching his lips, Windy bobbed his head in a nearly imperceptible greeting and Ramsey's hard eyes went back to Kincaid. "You can camp your troops here in the meadow if you want," he said. "There's water in the trough, grain in the barn. It's getting late in the day, so you might as well spend the night, if you want. When you get squared away, come on over to the big house. My sister will show you those papers."

As Ramsey limped toward the barn, Windy shifted in his saddle and dry leather creaked beneath him. "I think that young rooster needs his tail feathers plucked just a mite, Matthew."

"That he does, Windy, that he does. The right man will come along at the right time."

Windy grinned again, wider this time. "Maybe he already has."

Matt recognized the glint in the plainsman's eye. "Let's not get hasty, now, Windy. Remember, the man's offered us hospitality."

"I'll be sleepin' on God's ground, Matt. Ramsey's got no say over that."

"You old bastard," Kincaid muttered, stepping from his saddle and turning toward the command. "Lieutenant Davis?"

Davis stiffened to erect military posture in his saddle. "Yes, sir?"

"We'll bivouac here tonight, in that meadow well away from the buildings. Have the mounts watered here at the troughs, but feed them the army grain we brought with us. After grub, I want all weapons cleaned and inspected. Post a guard mount for tonight, and we're going to need a latrine trench dug." Kincaid watched the lieutenant momentarily. "Pick someone other than Private Radcliff," he added.

Davis' face tightened at the slight rebuke. "I'll see that it's done, sir. Do you have anyone in particular in mind for the latrine detail?" he asked, risking a touch of sarcasm in his tone.

"Yes, I have. But, military protocol won't allow it. Now get on with it, Lieutenant."

"Yes*sir*," Davis replied, wheeling his mount and saluting in one motion, not waiting for a response and leading the platoon toward the meadow.

Windy watched the young officer's retreating back. "Looks

like they've got one and we've got one, Matt."

"I'm afraid so, Windy," Matt replied, his cold eyes on the blue uniform. "But there's a difference; theirs, we've got to put up with. Ours, we don't. Lieutenant Davis!"

Davis held up his hand to halt the platoon, and turned his mount. "Sir?"

"I want you front and center over by that grove of trees in ten minutes!"

"Yes, sir. Will that be all, sir?"

"For the time being. Dismissed."

"Thank you, sir."

Again the platoon moved away, and Windy and Matt looked at each other.

"That's the trick, ain't it, Matt," Windy said. "To bring the man to heel without breakin' his spirit."

"True, Windy, very true. But that was supposed to have been done at the Academy. In the field there is no place for mavericks, whatever their rank. Either he comes around or I'll arrest him and put him under custody until we get back to the post."

"Wouldn't it do more good to just knock him on his ass a couple of times? The gettin' up part seems to be one hell of a fine teacher."

"I would prefer that myself. But between officers, matters of disagreement can't be handled that easily."

Kincaid leaned against a tree with his legs crossed, while chewing on a pine needle and tasting the bitterness of turpentine in his mouth, and watched Lieutenant Davis stride toward him. Matt had observed the young officer's efficient and rapid deployment of the platoon to the chores of the night's bivouac, and no matter how he tried, he couldn't dismiss the fact that he liked Davis in some strange way. There was a boyishness about him, like that of a youngster trying too hard to please his parents by doing everything right and, consequently, doing nearly everything wrong. When left to his own devices, though, away from the eyes of those whom he would impress, the true mettle of the young man's spirit is shown and he succeeds with ease, as had Davis in his handling of the platoon.

Matt folded his arms across his chest and watched Davis approach and stop five feet away. He snapped to attention with a muffled click of his heels in the grass and saluted crisply. "Lieutenant Davis reporting as ordered, sir."

Kincaid leaned away from the tree, straightened his body, returned the salute, and leaned back again to fold his arms across his chest once more. "At ease, Lieutenant."

Davis stepped sharply into the at-ease position with hands clasped behind his back, not looking at ease at all. He stared straight ahead, neither eyes nor head wavering right or left.

"I said at ease, Lieutenant," Matt growled. "I didn't say parade rest. Relax, dammit, I want to talk to you."

Davis shifted into what he hoped would please his superior and glanced warily toward Kincaid with a weak grin. "Sorry, sir."

"You're not sorry, Davis. You're stupid."

"Pardon me, sir?"

"You heard me. Sorry doesn't mean shit with dead men lying at your feet, and stupidity is guaranteed to produce dead soldiers."

Davis stared straight ahead again, remaining silent.

"What you did today was stupid, Davis, there's no other word for it. This is not West Point and you aren't moving little wooden armies around on a big tactical deployment board and playing war games. We are dealing with real people here. Real blood, real guts, and real letters to write to the parents of the dead in your command, if they happen to have any. Fortunately, few of them have anybody who gives a sorry damn about them. If they did, the way you're going you'd be spending most of your time writing letters."

A look of genuine confusion crossed Davis' face. "I'm sorry, sir. I don't understand."

Matt took a moment to think and realized for the first time that Davis was not even aware of what he had done wrong. He remembered his own first days with a Plains regiment, and suddenly he felt strangely weary of it all. He closed his eyes for a second, then opened them again to see Davis staring intently at his face.

"You're dismissed, Lieutenant," Matt said quietly.

"Sir?"

"I said you're dismissed."

"If you'll pardon my asking, sir, are you all right?"

"I'll not pardon your asking. I said you were dismissed."

"Certainly, sir. Thank you, sir," Davis said, snapping a hasty salute, which Kincaid returned without enthusiasm. Then the young lieutenant spun on his heel and moved out smartly in the direction of the encampment.

Matt leaned against the tree and watched the young man retreat.The shavetail's optimism was as yet undimmed, his beliefs untarnished, and his courage untested. He thought about himself. West Point, class of '69. Too late for the Civil War, but now on his second Western tour. Cited for bravery against the Comanche on the Staked Plains, and a veteran of countless battles and skirmishes, he had seen the brave, good men of both sides fall. Overage in grade, he should have been a captain long ago, but with the financial crunch the country was suffering under, he considered himself lucky even to get paid, much less promoted.

Matt hunched away from the tree and there was a bemused smile on his face as he watched Lieutenant Davis, now back at the encampment, snap an order at a soldier who had crossed an invisible line. *You're right, Windy,* Matt said to himself as he angled toward the main building of the Bucking R. *The spirit is the important thing. Break the spirit and you've broken the man. Common sense will teach him what he needs to know about survival on the Plains.*

When he passed by the main corral, he met young Ramsey leading a black stallion from the corral to the barn. "Nice-looking horse," Matt offered with sincerity. "Mind if I have a look?"

"Help yourself," Ramsey replied. "He's not quite as good as the roan yet, but he will be, with a little more work. Strong and quick." His eyes narrowed as he watched Kincaid. "A match for any Indian pony in the territory."

"Most grain-fed horses are, over the long haul," Matt said, ignoring the taunting remark and stooping to inspect the left front hoof. "But there aren't many that can touch them for that first burst of speed."

"You're speaking about those army plugs you're used to riding, Lieutenant. Old Sambo here's another story, in another class."

Matt finished his inspection and brushed the magnificent animal's neck and shoulders. "You're probably right, but don't let his speed serve only to have you be the first carried to his death in an ambush, Mr. Ramsey."

"Save your lectures for the boys in blue, Lieutenant."

"Consider them saved. You said I should see your sister about inspecting your grazing permits. Do you think she would be available to see me now?"

"Sure. Let me put old Sambo in his stall, then I'll introduce you to Betty Jo, or B.J., as I call her." Ramsey walked toward the barn and spoke over his shoulder as he moved. "I don't know which of those two names she hates the most, or if it's just me, but she's stuck with 'em, so why not like 'em? Be right with you, Lieutenant."

With the horse put away, they walked toward the big house and Ramsey talked cordially, as though they might be old friends. He was nearly Matt's height, but built light and quick, with sinewy muscle reminiscent of a snake coiled to strike.

"B.J.'s my older sister by four years, but you'd think she was my mother, the way she acts sometimes. Worry about this, worry about that. I tell you, Lieutenant, sometimes I wonder if she ain't gonna worry me to death with her worryin', instead of herself."

"Most women seem to be that way, for a fact," Matt said with a chuckle.

"I take too many chances, I drink too much . . . God! On and on it goes. Cattle prices are down, we're losing too much stock, I'm gonna get killed and leave her by herself . . ."

"By herself?" Matt asked as they neared the porch. "Are just she and yourself running this spread?"

"Yeah, with the exception of Ernie and the hands. Pa built this place up and was killed in an Indian raid for his troubles. There." Ramsey pointed toward a corner wall of the building. "See those charred logs? Fire arrows. Tried to burn the place down, but Pa and the hands saved it. Then he bled to death. He left it to me and Betty Jo. B.J. and her husband came up from Texas to run it a few years ago, and I came along a little later. Then her husband died—pneumonia—and it's been just me and her ever since."

"Sorry to hear about that," Matt said sincerely, as their boots thudded on the front steps.

"That's the way it goes. Maybe you can understand now why I don't have a helluva lot of love for featherheads."

"There's been a few of them killed in the course of this thing, too, Mr. Ramsey."

Young Ramsey stopped with his hand on the screen door, and turned toward Matt. "Do me two favors, will you, Lieutenant? First, lay off the lectures with me. Second, call me Dave. A man half again as old as I am callin' me 'mister' makes me nervous. Come on in. I'll rustle up B.J., then pour us a drink. You a whiskey man?"

"I've been known to drink my share when the occasion is right."

"Is the occasion right?"

"It might be, at that."

Ramsey grinned an easy, carefree grin. "That's what I like to hear. You might not be such a bad sort after all, know that, Lieutenant?"

"There are those who would argue that point with you, Dave," Matt replied, removing his hat as they stepped inside.

With one glance, Matt could immediately see that the Ramsey home had been built for both comfort and durability. The walls of the spacious living room, constructed of heavy logs chinked against the winter winds, were covered with rough-cut knotty pine and draped with rugs, skins, and furs. The soft yellow of the wood was made even softer by the reds and browns of couches and chairs and the oval, braided rug in the center of the room. A massive flagstone fireplace filled one entire corner of the room, and off to the right Matt could see the entranceway into a comfortable, well-appointed kitchen. To the left was an arched opening leading to the bedrooms and offices. The windows were heavily shuttered and spaced at wide intervals throughout. Rifle ports had been cut into the walls, allowing, Matt assumed, for the successful defense of the Bucking R ranch in which the elder Mr. Ramsey had lost his life.

The clink of glass against glass brought Kincaid from his reverie and he turned to see young Ramsey approaching with a glass in either hand, one of which he handed to the officer. "I decided to change the order of business a little bit," Ramsey allowed with a grin. "First we'll have a drink, then we'll call B.J."

"Whatever's fair. Here's to your health," Matt replied, raising his glass and extending it toward Ramsey before drinking. Ramsey matched the motion and savored the taste of whiskey as it eased slowly down his throat.

"Lord God, that's good stuff!" Ramsey wheezed, sucking in a breath and holding it.

"Either cure you or kill you, won't it?" Matt managed, blinking at the film of moisture filling his eyes.

"Have you found a new playmate, David?" asked a feminine voice from somewhere beneath the archway.

Matt's back was turned toward the archway, and he noticed

young Ramsey's face as he turned in mild surprise. There was a devilish grin on the cattleman's lips, as though he were pleased to have irritated his sister in some small way.

"Ah, the beauteous and fair B.J. Ramsey makes her grand appearance," Ramsey said mockingly. "In answer to your question, my dear, I'm not really certain if I'm drinking with friend or foe. But, with time and good whiskey, all things will out. B.J., meet an honored guest and one who suspects us of treachery. Lieutenant Kincaid, my sister Betty Jo. B.J., meet the savior of the nation."

Matt was turning toward the archway as Ramsey spoke, and he stopped, stunned, as he faced Betty Jo Ramsey. It was easily apparent that David Ramsey's handsomeness was a product of heredity. Where he was handsome, his sister was beautiful, and they might have been twins, were it not for the age difference. Her long, soft blond hair hung in a twist across her left shoulder and nearly touched her waist as it draped in an enticing bulge over a full breast. Fathomless eyes of the darkest green were accented by a deeply tanned face, with high cheekbones narrowing to full lips now slightly parted over perfectly constructed, flawlessly white teeth. Her floor-length dress was made of soft blue material, and the tanned skin below her throat was revealed through a square opening in the bodice, which allowed a hint of cleavage to show. Her waist appeared to Matt to be no bigger than the circumference of two hands pressed together in a circle.

Matt reddened at the neckline when he realized he was staring, and he smiled in apology. "I'm sorry. I think you caught me unawares. It's a real pleasure to meet you, Miss Ramsey."

Betty Jo dipped into a half-curtsey. "The pleasure is mine, Lieutenant. To what do we owe the honor of a visit from the United States Army?"

"Primarily, we're here to check out a rumor that . . ."

The whiskey bottle touched glass and Ramsey poured again as he interrupted Matt. "That we're grazing our cattle illegally on Injun land. He wants to see our permits." Ramsey smiled at Kincaid. "Isn't that correct, Lieutenant? To your health, sir," he concluded, draining his glass in a single gulp while Matt took his down halfway.

A look of mild irritation crossed Betty Jo's face as she looked at her brother, then back at Matt. "I assure you that our papers are in order, Lieutenant Kincaid. I'll get them for you if you wish."

"There's no great hurry, Miss—"

"Betty Jo," she corrected him.

"Very well, and you must call me Matt, then."

She smiled, and there was a hint of mystery in her eyes. "Matt."

"Agreed. There's no great hurry, Betty Jo. Whenever . . ."

"Hell no, there's no hurry," Ramsey interrupted. "Come on, let's sit down and have a drink."

"When it's time for a drink, you'll always be the first man there, won't you, David?" Betty Jo asked with resignation in her voice.

"You're damned right I will be," David responded hotly, moving forward with the bottle once more. His limp was obvious now.

"You're hurt, David," Betty Jo said, moving forward instinctively while pressing her hands against her thighs.

Ramsey poured into Matt's glass and filled his own again. "Nothin' to it, big sister. Horse fell. Broke a leg and had to be destroyed. I got a little sprained knee, that's all."

Matt watched the young cattleman's eyes and saw no indication that he was lying. Their eyes met, and Ramsey's seemed to glaze over as he stared at Kincaid.

"Ain't that a fact, Lieutenant? You fellers came along just after it happened."

Matt hesitated momentarily. "Yes, that's the way it appeared to me. Mighty fine horse. Shame to see it get killed that way."

"Yup, shame it is. But that's life . . . or death. Come on, let's sit down a spell. Can I get you a drink, Betty Jo?"

"Yes, David," Betty Jo responded, taking a seat on the edge of the sofa. "A brandy, please." She watched Kincaid for a change in expression, and found none. "While my brother is occupied with that chore, Matt, finish telling me what brings you and yours to the northern Plains."

"Certainly. We're quartered at Outpost Number Nine, about two days' hard riding to the south. A trapper named Seth Daniels made a point of stopping by the post to pass along some disturbing news he'd heard about the Arapaho. According to my chief scout, Windy Mandalian, Daniels is the virtual paragon of honesty and he said that a medicine man named

Gray Bear was in the process of whipping these Arapaho into a war-fever again. Have either of you heard anything about that?"

David handed the brandy to his sister, took a seat beside her, and nodded grimly. "Yeah, I have. Did this Daniels of yours say anything about green arrows as far as the eye can see and returning to the old ways before the white man?"

"Yes, he did. Almost those words exactly, as a matter of fact."

Ramsey nodded again. "If my memory is correct, and I know damned well it is, green is the color of their war arrows, and they were some of the meanest, scalp-takin'est sons of bitches in the country before the white man came. And after, too, for that matter. I, for one, ain't real anxious to see them go back to the way they were before we came to these parts, but if they're askin' for a butt-kickin' again, we're more than ready to give it to them."

Kincaid studied the grim look on young Ramsey's face, and he knew the ringing sound of determination in his words was for real. He wondered how many other cattlemen in the area felt the same way.

"Well, unless you're attacked, it's a military problem for right now," Matt said. "We'll be on our way over to the agency in the morning to talk with the man from the Bureau of Indian Affairs. He should know more about this than we do, and maybe the whole thing is a misunderstanding." Matt sipped his whiskey and contemplated his glass. "Then again, maybe it's not."

The setting sun cast a crimson glow through the living room, and shafts of diffused light pierced the room. The setting seemed to control the mood and held them in mutual contemplation for long moments until Betty Jo finally broke the silence with a near-whisper. "I hope nothing bad happens again. I wish we could live with them in peace."

Ramsey placed his arm around her shoulders and hugged her lightly. "Honey, you know better than that. They're savages, always have been and always will be. The only peace they know is a piece of white man's hair hanging from a coup stick."

"David, you're judging a whole race of people on what a few—" Matt began.

"I'm judging the bastards that killed our pa! He wasn't

causin' them no trouble, but that didn't stop the arrow, a *green* arrow, from goin' through his stomach. I haven't had a chance to pay any of 'em back yet for what they done, but maybe my day's comin'."

Matt listened to Ramsey's words and could hear a drunken slur beginning to mold them into a continuous drone. A wild look had come into his eyes, and he lurched to his feet and snatched the whiskey bottle from the shelf.

"Where are you going, David?" Betty Jo asked.

"To the bunkhouse. The boys are havin' a poker game tonight and I'm gonna sit in awhile. I'll eat with them and bunk out there, so don't, for God's sake, worry about my not comin' back. 'Night, sis."

After David had gone, Matt and Betty Jo sat in the living room surrounded by a strained silence. Finally she sipped her brandy and looked across at Matt.

"Don't judge David too harshly, Matt. He's young and he's wild, but he's also got a heart of gold. The hands think the world of him and would do anything for him, as would he for them. He hasn't quite gotten over our father's death."

"Where was David when the attack occurred?"

"China."

"China?"

"Yes, China. Our father owned a ranch in Texas before we came here, but his father, our grandfather, was a sea captain. David was raised on the ranch and learned all there was to know about running a cattle spread, but he had a wanderlust, a desire to see other places. So he hired out on our grandfather's ship and sailed before the mast for two years. When they came home from that first voyage, he learned of our father's death. The one person, with the exception of Grampa, whom he loved and looked up to was gone. He's still burning for revenge."

"He seems like a very aggressive young man. If that aggressiveness is channeled in the right direction, it could be a benefit to him instead of a liability."

Betty Jo sipped her brandy and watched Kincaid over the rim of the snifter. "Don't take David lightly in any regard, Matt, especially physical confrontation. He was a different person when he came back from his voyage. He was no longer the happy-go-lucky young man who fought, drank, and raised hell just because he was glad to be alive. He learned some things in the Orient, and aboard ship I suppose, that most other men don't know. Now, when he fights, he is deadly; when he drinks, he becomes morose and seems to relive a nightmare from somewhere in his past. He frightens me sometimes, and I'm the only person in the world he loves. Imagine what he would be like to an enemy or a stranger."

"Thank you for the warning, Betty Jo. I have no desire for a confrontation with David on any level. I have a job to do, and regardless of David or anyone else, I'll see that the job gets done properly." Matt drained the whiskey and placed his glass carefully on a table while watching Betty Jo with a pleasant smile on his face. "And speaking of responsibility, I suppose I had better see that my men have been properly cared for. Would it be any trouble for you to show me those grazing permits before I go?"

Betty Jo did not respond, choosing instead to watch him in the closing twilight that filled the room with a strange melancholy, presaging the aloneness of the coming night. Their eyes held each other, and she absentmindedly caressed the rim of her brandy snifter with full lips slightly parted and the tip of her tongue trailing across the cool glass. And when she finally spoke, there was a huskiness to her voice.

"You haven't eaten supper, have you, Lieutenant?"

"No. No, I haven't. I can get something from the mess sergeant when I get down to our bivouac area."

"Would you do me the honor of dining with me this evening?" she asked, continuing to watch him like a beautiful cat, with her green eyes catching the last rays of the dying sun.

"Thank you, no. I couldn't put you to the trouble."

"It would be no trouble. It would be a pleasure. I'll fix supper, and the cook can have the evening to herself."

"Well, if you're sure . . ."

"I'm sure." Her voice was filled with enthusiasm now, like a little girl who had suddenly received an unexpected present wrapped in beautiful ribbons and bows. "It will be fun. You go down and check on your men, or whatever you have to do, and I'll get dinner started. On your way by, I'll ask you to lower a bottle of wine into the well to cool, and we'll dine by candlelight. Surely a soldier could stand a break from routine just as much as a reluctant cattle baroness?"

Matt's soft chuckle was filled with contented warmth. "Without a doubt, Betty Jo. It sounds delightful. You get the wine and I'll take care of the rest."

• • •

As he turned the crank and reeled the oaken bucket up from the depths of the well, Matt felt a thrill of excitement pass through his lean, muscular frame. His skin felt alive from the recent shave and splash of cologne, the clean shirt felt good across his broad shoulders, and the rising evening breeze ruffled the freshly combed hair around the edges of his just-brushed campaign hat. He had been pleased with Lieutenant Davis' handling of night encampment, particularly when the posted guard had asked for the password, which he didn't know. He had not seen Windy Mandalian, but that didn't strike him as unusual. The scout seldom spent his nights with troops bivouacked in the field, preferring instead to trust to his own devices and senses on the open plains.

Matt felt an aura of contentment when his hand closed around the neck of the cool bottle and he stepped toward the porch. As he reached for the door, he started to knock, hesitated, then stepped inside. The mellow glow of lamps turned low filled the living room with a warmth which was enhanced by the crackling of a small fire in the fireplace to ward off the coming chill of night.

He could smell a delectable aroma drifting from the kitchen, and the sound of something sizzling in a frying pan reached his ears. Stepping quietly into the kitchen, he saw Betty Jo standing before the range with an apron tied around her waist. She was humming a soft melody.

"The wine seems to have chilled very nicely," he said, hoping not to startle her.

She turned to face him. There was a radiance about her face, a pinkness in her cheeks from the heat of the stove; a glow of vitality filled her eyes. "I'm glad," she said. "That is supposed to be a very nice wine, although I'll have to admit I'm no connoisseur. But my father was, and that bottle is from his cellar, so we'll have to say it's good, whether it is or not. I hope you like mountain quail. I thought it might be a nice change for you from beef."

"Anything will be a nice change from beef, and I'm sure whatever you're preparing will be excellent. Like yourself, I know nothing about wine and I've never tasted quail, so I'm completely at your mercy."

Betty Jo chuckled her pleasure. "Good, then we'll dine in

ignorance. Go pour yourself a drink if you'd like, and as soon as I can let these simmer, I'll join you by the fireplace."

"Fine. May I get you anything?" Matt asked, turning toward the living room.

"Yes, please. I think I can handle another small brandy without it going to my head too badly."

Matt was seated by the fireplace, whiskey in hand, staring into the flames licking the edges of the fresh log he had thrown on the fire, when Betty Jo came into the room. He heard the rustle of paper and glanced up to see her stop behind him and study the two documents in her hands briefly.

"These are the grazing permits," she said, handing them down across Matt's left shoulder. "I thought it would be nice to get our business out of the way before dinner."

Matt looked up at her as he received the papers. "Actually, I feel a little embarrassed even to have to check them. Your kindness and hospitality has me a bit overwhelmed." He paused and watched her closely. "Not to mention your beauty."

A tiny blush crept into her cheeks and she smiled self-consciously. "Nonsense. You came here to do your job and I'm sure you couldn't leave without having done it. So let's get it over with."

Matt nodded, taking the papers and holding them toward the lamplight. He read the two documents rapidly, then shifted back and forth from paper to paper in search of the name of the person to whom they had been issued. Betty Jo leaned down to help him, and her right breast pressed firmly against his left shoulder just as Matt turned to ask where the name might be. Their faces were but inches apart. He could smell the fragrance of her hair. They were frozen in place, lips parted and eyes intertwined. Matt lifted his mouth toward hers and their lips barely touched before she pulled away with a nervous adjustment of her apron.

"The papers were issued to my father, and his name is on the back of each. My brother and I have legal right to the permits as a condition of his will," she said quickly as she stepped toward the kitchen. There was a stammer in her voice. "I'd . . . I'd . . . better check on supper, it should be nearly ready."

The quail, rolled in flour and dipped in egg batter, could not have been more succulent, and, complemented by creamed peas, boiled potatoes with gravy, and freshly baked bread, their meal was a combination of flavors that left nothing to be desired. The wine, a Riesling imported from Germany, was just dry enough to cleanse the palate, yet sufficiently sweet to provide pleasant flavor. The candles in the darkened room cast long shadows upon the wall and they talked softly about the past, as though the slightest alien sound might destroy the mood. Their hands touched occasionally in exchange of a dish or other object, and one's eyes seldom strayed from the other's face. There was a communication between them that words could not have expressed, and which, if attempted, would surely have spoiled the moment.

When their dinner was over, they moved again to the fireplace to finish their wine. Matt threw a fresh log on the fire, then sank down on the couch beside Betty Jo. She made no attempt to move away; their thighs touched full length and there was an instant warmth communicated beteween them. Matt offered his glass toward hers in salute and she watched him as he leaned toward her, his lips closing on hers. When their lips first touched, there was no movement, no indication of pleasure. Then, slowly, gently, their mouths began a probing, testing quest to search out every feeling, every hidden sensation, and their breathing became faster, and when Matt placed his arm around her and pulled her to him he could feel the pounding of her heart against his chest. With his free hand he placed the wine glasses on the end table, while her hands went to the back of his head and then to his hair. She caught a sharp half-breath, and a tiny moan escaped her lips as she pressed her mouth even more hungrily against his.

He began to explore her body with his left hand while his right moved into silky, golden hair. Her body arched against his hand when he touched her breast, and he could feel the full firmness of her and the hardening dot in the center of his palm. Her mouth moved to his ear and she whispered to him through a searching, tongue-probing kiss. "It's been so long, Matt, it's been so long. No man has touched me since my husband died, and that's been nearly two years. Please be gentle with me, but love me. Love me good and love me hard, but be gentle with me. I love you for tonight, just for tonight, but I love you tonight. Love me, make love to me and love me."

There was trembling in his knees when Matt stood and carried her in his arms to the thick bearskin rug before the fireplace. Their lips never parted and their kiss continued as he lowered her to her feet and loosened the top buttons on the bodice of her dress. She shivered beneath his hands and kicked off her shoes to stand barefooted in the thick hair of the rug, which went between her toes and created an unusual sensation she had never felt before. Like many women in this part of the country at this time, she wore no corsets, and when her dress and shift slipped to her hips, then to encircle her feet, Matt stood slightly back and looked at her.

She made no attempt to cover herself and she knew no shame nor embarrassment. Her breasts arched toward him with nipples firm and full, and the golden hair of her pubic region glistened, taking on a reddish-brown hue in the firelight. Taking her breasts in either hand, he kissed and fondled them individually and she closed her eyes with head thrown back and her breathing was ragged now.

"You're the most beautiful woman I've ever known, Betty Jo," he whispered as he gently lowered her to the rug. "I want to love you. If only for tonight, I want to hold you and make love to you and love you."

And then they were together, separated from the world, alone in the universe. The candles went out and the fire dimmed to nothing but red-hot coals, and for a timeless hour they held each other and loved, until it was time for Matt to return to his command. But they had taken heat from each other, and it warmed them through what remained of the chill night.

four

"I don't give a goddamn what you say you heard, Lieutenant, I can't believe that Gray Bear would incite his people to engage in another war!" The Indian agent, Doug Collins, tugged at his sagging pants and tried to pull the strained material up over his drooping stomach. Abandoning the task, he lit his small cigar, poured another shot of whiskey, and looked at Windy Mandalian and Kincaid once again. "Sure, I've heard those rumors myself about going back to the old way, and green arrows farther than a goddamned crow can fly, but I don't pay 'em no mind. I'm convinced there ain't a man alive who can understand, much less know, what these Arapaho are talking about, and that includes most Arapaho. They're kind of a sneaky bunch anyhow, and aren't too long on matching straight answers to straight questions."

Windy smiled and turned the whiskey glass in his fingertips. "You got that right, Doug. They'd climb a tree to tell you a lie when standin' on the ground and tellin' the truth'd do 'em more good." Windy looked at Matt, who had declined the agent's offer of a drink. "What's the matter with you, Matt? Work a little too hard last night?"

Ignoring the remark, Matt concentrated on the Indian agent, although a corner of his mind kept wandering to another place, another time. "I admire your defense of these Arapaho, Doug, and your effort to provide them with the goods and services the government has promised them. A lot of agents aren't that dedicated."

"Hell, I ain't dedicated, Matt. Just tryin' to do a job. Most of these people are thinking more about food and shelter than counting coup and returning to any form of warfare with the white man. They are a beaten people who—and I'm sure Gray Bear fits into this category—wish only to live in peace now. There are some young bucks, Eagle Flies Alone is the first who comes to mind, who would like to make a name for themselves and see the tribe return to the warpath. Of course there are quite a few young hotheads who think like he does and are willing to join him, but by and large, most of the tribe I'm sure would rather live in peace."

"I wish I could be totally certain of that, Doug, but I can't. What do you make of those three warriors we saw decked out in their warpaint? With the claim Gray Bear is supposed to be making, and seeing Arapaho on the warpath myself, there's just too much evidence against these people to forget the whole damned thing. How long has it been since you've seen Gray Bear?"

"When I first heard these rumors, oh, about three weeks ago, I asked Gray Bear to come to me so we could talk. You know the Indian mind, Windy, and so do you, Matt; they'll come, but only when they get damned well good and ready. Well, anyway, he finally showed up sometime last week and I asked him about it. His English is just a little worse than my Arapaho, so, as you can imagine, we weren't getting a hell of a lot accomplished. The only interpreter I could find was Lame Crow, a young buck with a leg that was fucked up when he was born, so he's pissed off at the world anyway and he's one of Eagle Flies Alone's cronies.

"I asked my questions and Lame Crow passed them along, or at least I thought that was what he was doing. But the old man seemed to keep getting more confused, even worse than when I was talking to him in English. The kid kept saying Gray Bear didn't understand why I would accuse him of doing something wrong, and I kept saying I wasn't accusing him, only trying to get a clear story. It all came to nothing, with the old man leaving here shaking his head and grunting. I haven't seen him since, but when I asked about him I was told he had gone to the mountain to seek a vision." The agent snorted and reached for his glass again. "If that ain't a crock of shit. You can dress 'em up in white man's clothes and feed 'em pork and beans till it runs out their ears, but you'll never change their way of thinkin' in a million years."

"Unfortunately, we don't have that long, Doug," Matt said as he turned to Windy. "What part of the Rockies do you think Gray Bear was referring to when he said he was going to the mountains, Windy?"

"Can't say for sure, Matt, but if I wanted real bad to try and find him, I'd start looking somewhere in the Bald Rock area. Some of the medicine men around here seem to think it's a spirit place; maybe Gray Bear does too. Be damned tough, though, findin' an Arapaho, especially one as old and wise as Gray Bear, on his own ground."

"We haven't got any choice, Windy. We have to know for certain what the meaning is of what he's telling his people. It appears to me that Gray Bear himself is the only one who can tell us that for sure. If we find him, can you speak enough Arapaho for our needs?"

"Don't know. Haven't tried it yet."

"You can speak some, though?"

"Some. It's Algonquin, like Cheyenne, but a mite more complicated."

"Well, we'll have to give it a try and we haven't got time to hunt up an interpreter, even if we could find one we could trust."

The Indian agent followed them to the door and they shook hands all around. "Thanks a lot, Doug," Matt said. "I'm going to leave two squads of the platoon here, just in case things go to hell, and take the third squad with Windy and me to find Gray Bear. We should be back in a couple of days. Lieutenant Davis will be in charge of the detachment left here, and I'll instruct him to cooperate with you in any way possible."

"Thanks, Matt. I don't think we'll need any protection, but better safe than sorry, I guess."

"That's what they way. See you when we get back."

The platoon had been dismissed to await the adjutant's return, and now, as Lieutenant Davis saw Kincaid walking toward them, he scrambled to his feet and snapped into a ramrod posture, yelling, "P'*toon*, tenn-*shutt*!"

Unused to military protocol in the field, the soldiers were slow in gaining the position of attention desired by Lieutenant Davis, and he turned on them with a withering gaze. "Now, goddammit! When I call you to attention I want it today, not tomorrow or next Sunday!"

By the time Kincaid arrived, the men were in a scattered formation but standing stiffly at attention. He wanted to laugh but he knew he couldn't, and when he looked at several of his seasoned veterans, like Platoon Sergeant Gus Olsen in particular, he knew what was going through their minds. Something like, "Where the fuck did this asshole come from and when, for Christsakes, is he leaving again?"

"At ease, men," Matt said. "Lieutenant Davis, I'd like to speak to you alone for a moment, please. Corporal Wojensky? Have your squad fall into ranks and prepare to move out."

Matt moved several feet away, with Davis following, and when he stopped and turned, Davis stepped into his starched, parade-rest stance. Kincaid shook his head but made no comment.

"Lieutenant Davis, Windy and I are going to take Third Squad and go into the mountains and try to find an old medicine man named Gray Bear. He's the only one who knows for certain what the Arapaho have in mind. I want you to stay here with the remainder of the platoon and keep an eye on the agency just in case things get out of hand around here before we get back, which should be in a couple of days. The agent's name is Doug Collins and I want you to cooperate with him in every way. Are there any questions?"

"No, sir. I am to defend the lives and property of this government installation and those assigned here. That's fairly clear, isn't it, sir?"

Matt nodded with a resigned sigh. "Yeah, I guess that's the same as keeping an eye on things. Sergeant Olsen is a good man and a seasoned veteran. Don't hesitate to ask his opinion if you need some advice."

"Thank you, sir, but I won't be needing any advice. Have a good patrol."

"Thank you, Lieutenant," Matt said, returning the crisp salute and shaking his head as he walked toward the mounted squad waiting in the middle of the street, with Windy Mandalian slouching in his saddle at the head of the column. At six foot seven, one squad member, Private Stretch Dobbs, loomed over his fellow soldiers like a naked flagpole and Kincaid wondered how God could have inflicted so much clumsiness, size, ignorance, and good intentions on just one human being.

Taking up the reins, Matt swung into the saddle and led the column away from the agency. Several Arapaho, mostly old or crippled, hung around the shade of the buildings where white traders bargained with domestic goods and baubles for whatever goods the Indians had to trade. He felt a strange uneasiness about leaving Davis in charge of the remaining two squads and the safety of the agency, and would have much preferred to have Sergeant Gus Olsen responsible for the platoon, but the chain of command did not allow for noncoms to order officers around.

Sensing Matt's unsettled thoughts, Windy bit off a chew of tobacco, nestled the cut in his cheek, worked up some flavor, and spat.

"Gotta let him try it on his own sometime, Matt. Might as well let it be now, while it don't look like there's too much he can fuck up."

"Yeah, you're right, Windy," Matt replied, trying to relax and failing. "Guess all generals were second lieutenants at one time, huh?"

"Yup. Hard to tell the difference 'tween 'em."

Matt threw his head back and laughed, and he felt better for just being away from the agency and Lieutenant Davis.

By late afternoon they had left the prairie grassland behind, and climbed through the thick stands of yellow pine, hemlock, spruce, and fir, which yielded to stunted, gnarled cedar and pine on the lower slopes of the Rockies. Trees deformed by wind, heavy snow, and avalanches stood among the boulders like silent sentinels, warning trespassers of the region's treacherousness, and the increasing wind whistling down the slopes seemed to cry out for all intruders to go back, and not to violate the sanctity of the spirits residing in their silent world of raw, naked beauty.

When night fell, they bivouacked in the upper reaches of a huge bowl, and as they looked to the south, the uniformity of the timber made it appear as though they were looking upon a green sea. The treetops rolled in constant waves, bending to their limits, then rocking back to be taken by the wind again. There was a loneliness about the sights and sounds around them. Matt filled his coffee mug again and reached over to refill Windy's, and said, "Doesn't it seem a bit peculiar for a senile old Indian to be up here alone, searching for guidance and wisdom to lead his people on the proper path? Seems to me that would be the job for a young man, if this is the only place that inspiration can be found."

"You saw what the young ones are doin', Matt," Windy replied, blowing on his tin cup to cool the steaming coffee. "Paintin' themselves up for war. I don't know if it's because of what the old man said, but if it is, I'll bet my last plug of tobacco that it's because that's what they wanted to hear. If

Gray Bear is for a fact tryin' to get them back on the warpath again, he wouldn't need to come *here* to palaver with his gods. He would have done it at home."

"Then you figure if anything is going to happen, it's going to happen with or without Gray Bear?"

"That's what I've been figurin' most of the afternoon. We haven't picked up any sign of him today, even though he's probably seen us a dozen times or more, and I don't think we'll do much better tomorrow. Tryin' to catch an Arapaho who's spent his entire life in these hills is kinda like a dog tryin' to catch its tail; he might be able to see it, but he'll never get his teeth into it."

Matt sloshed the coffee around the sides of his mug and watched the strong brown liquid lap the edges. "Think we'd better get back to the agency before too long? Maybe it was a little bit stupid of me to come up here in the first place. I didn't think we had a hell of a lot of chance of finding him, but I did think that maybe he would want to come out and talk if he had no desire for war."

"It wasn't stupid, Matt. I thought the same thing. Besides, a man's gotta *do* somethin' sometimes, even if it's wrong. You didn't have much choice."

"I know. But to tell you the truth, what's really eating me is the thought of leaving two squads of good men in a vulnerable position."

"If they're good men, you don't have anything to worry about."

"A team of horses, no matter what the quality of the animals, is only as good as the man holding the reins, Windy, my friend. Same goes for a military outfit."

Windy took a final sip of his coffee, tossed the remains away, leaned back against his saddle, and tilted the hat over his eyes. "Best find out now, before you have to trust a flank to him someday. 'Night."

"Good night, you pragmatic, insufferable old bastard," Matt mumbled with a grin. He pulled his blankets up to his chest, yawned, then said in a sleepy voice, "Since we rode all the way up here, let's look around until about noon and then head back. I'd still like to find Gray Bear and get to the bottom of this if we can, but if we can't, that should put us back at the agency before nightfall. How's that to you?"

The answer was a gentle snoring coming from beneath Windy's hat.

Lieutenant Davis moved quietly through the darkness toward the sentry silhouetted against the weak light of the horizon. He felt good, supercharged with energy. At last he was in command in the field, with no senior officers around. It gave him a pleasurable feeling of power, as though finally all those years at West Point were paying off. And now he would try to slip past his own sentry to see if he was alert, and God help him if he wasn't. He paused by the agency office then, and as the soldier turned to retrace the route of his guard post, Davis moved forward in a hunched-over, running position. He had traveled nearly twenty yards unchallenged, and he knew he would make it past the sentry. There would be a lesson learned this night.

"Halt!"

The lieutenant continued to move.

"I said halt, goddammit, or I'll give ya a new asshole!"

There was a ringing sound of authority in the soldier's voice, one that the lieutenant decided it would be best not to ignore. He froze in his tracks.

"That's better, ya goofy bastard! Now get flat on your face in the dirt!"

Davis glanced warily over his shoulder, afraid to move abruptly. "There's no need for that, soldier. It's me, Lieutenant Davis."

"Lieutenant Davis, the man says! Lieutenant Davis, my ass! He's got no reason to be sneakin' around here in the middle of the night. On your belly, mister, or I'll put you on your back!"

A slow smolder began in Davis' mind and became a raging inferno across the surface of his brain. "You know it's me, Radcliff, goddammit! Now cut out the bullshit and let me go back to the command."

Davis thought he heard a low chuckle.

"I don't know nothin', mister. I'm just a soldier on guard mount, and I'm mighty experienced at that, as you might know, and I have to exercise my own best judgment when it comes to infiltrators. I have the right to shoot. My judgment is that you get flat on your fucking belly or I'm going to use that right!"

Davis knew he was trapped, but he thought he'd try one last out. "The password is 'snowbird.' Now I'm ordering you to let me go."

"You ain't orderin' anybody, mister. That password ain't no good unless I have cause to believe you're a friendly, which cause I ain't got yet. Now, one last time, before I lose my patience, on your fucking belly in the dirt. Now!"

Lieutenant Davis dropped to his knees, then flopped to his stomach in the thick dust.

"Sergeant of the Guard!" Radcliff screamed, although he knew Gus Olsen stood no more than ten yards away.

Olsen waited what he figured was a judicious length of time, then moved forward at a shuffling run. "Yeah, Private. What is it?"

"Infiltrator, Sarge. Watch my post and I'll go forward to take him prisoner."

"Go ahead, soldier. And good work."

"Thanks, Sarge. Every minute of it a pleasure."

With his rifle extended and prepared to fire, Radcliff moved toward the dark figure lying facedown in the dust. He approached David from behind, jerked the lieutenant's hands to the small of his back, then pressed the muzzle of his rifle against the nape of his neck.

"You, my friend, have just been taken captive," he said, the pleasure evident in his voice.

Davis twisted on his side, oblivious of the Springfield, and stared up at Radcliff. "It's me, Lieutenant Davis, you dumb bastard! Now knock off the horseshit or I'll have you court-martialed and hung!"

Radcliff smiled in the darkness and exclaimed innocently, "Well, I'll be go to hell! It *is* you, Lieutenant. What the hell you doin' sneakin' around out here in the middle of the night? Lose somethin'?"

Davis scrambled to his feet and brushed the dust from his forage blues with infuriated slaps. "Never you mind what I'm doing here, soldier! Get back to your post and I don't want to hear a word about this in the morning."

"My lips are sealed," Radcliff replied with a grin. "Want to change the password, sir? You said it pretty loud, might of got to the wrong ears."

Davis' lips curled into a snarl. "Didn't work for *me*, goddammit, why should it work for anyone else? Leave the son of a bitch the way it was and get back to your post!"

"Yessir," Radcliff said, backing away. "Love to. Please be careful around here at night, sir. Somebody might shoot you . . . by mistake."

Ignoring the remark, Lieutenant Davis stalked back to the encampment.

five

They were silhouetted against the pink morning sky, and there were sixty of them. Lean, brown, stripped to the waist in defiance of the morning chill, with stoic eyes and expressionless faces they watched the agency from atop a rolling swale. Young braves, all of them, none having gone beyond his twenty-fifth year, they sat their ponies with restless pride and held their rifles across their laps, loaded and ready. The majority of them were armed with the newer Spencer repeating rifle, prized weapons captured during the victory at the Little Big Horn and other, minor skirmishes, and never turned in with the signing of the truce, while the remaining few were equipped with single-shot Springfields. Certain of them had quivers hanging from their waists and lashed to empty coup belts, which were filled with arrows: the green-striped arrows of the Arapaho warrior.

Eagle Flies Alone sat his mount in the center and slightly to the front of the others. A Spencer was clutched in his left hand, while his right was raised and pointing toward the main street leading into the agency. Muscles rippled under his bronzed skin.

"Look at them," he said, barely controlling the rage in his voice. "Our people coming to be fed like animals by their master."

There was a chorus of sullen agreement behind him, and all eyes watched the procession of Arapaho tribesmen and their families journeying to the agency for their monthly ration of flour, salt, coffee, sugar, and sundry staples issued on the first of each month, when they were available. Many wore mixed dress, consisting of black, wide-brimmed hats, gaudy shirts, and fringed buckskin pants. Among them were some of the finest, fiercest, and proudest warriors of the Arapaho nation before the peace, now relegated to subsistence on the white man's dole. They rode, or walked, with heads held erect, but without arogance, pride, or passion.

"Here me, my brothers," Eagle Flies Alone began again, his tone firm and confident. "They are beaten, slaves of the white man. But we are not, and we must show them the path back to the ways of the Shining Times, just as old Gray Bear says, but not in the way of his meaning. We must hunt again, and raid upon the Utes and take their horses and women and make them ours." His expression turned as cold as his face. "We must kill the white man and drive him from our land. And the blond-haired one shall be first and his sister shall be mine. He had good fortune yesterday in the ravine, but he can't trust his life to luck forever. I have spoken."

Another warrior, Little Fox, nudged his pony up beside that of Eagle Flies Alone. "Where will Lame Crow and the others wait for the big soldier and his men? If we are to be successful here, he and the wolf in buckskin clothes must be stopped."

"You mean the scout, Mandalian? Yes, his reputation as a great warrior is well known. But Lame Crow will wait for them at Three Trees, the narrow trail through which they must pass. He has eight warriors and our best rifles. He cannot fail."

"That is good. I long for battle and my weapons thirst for the taste of blue-leg blood."

Eagle Flies Alone turned and clapped Little Fox between the shoulder blades, then grasped his arm just above the beadwork bracelet encircling his bicep. "You are a true friend and a valiant warrior, Little Fox. We will both be chiefs one day and our people will listen to us and respect us. We will have great face when we count coup on the Americans. And when we have destroyed their agency and all the food that enslaves our people, the strong of our tribe will follow us onto the Plains and the weak will die, as they should."

The sun was well above the horizon now, and the shadows stretched long and black behind Sergeant Olsen as he shielded his eyes and watched the warriors up on the ridge turn their mounts and move in a cluster toward the prairie floor.

"Lieutenant! Indians comin'!"

With some reluctance, Lieutenant Davis quit his rifle inspection and moved toward the sergeant. "What do you mean, 'Indians coming,' Sergeant? There are enough Indians here now to cover the better part of Vermont."

"I mean those Indians, sir," Olsen said, pointing toward the ridge. "I think they've got different plans than the ones already here."

Davis looked in the direction indicated, and a sly, almost pleased look crossed his face as he said, "Well, look there, would you. Maybe we just might see some action after all."

"I don't think you'll see any action from this visit, sir. They'll blow off steam, and then, if they think they can pull it off, they just might attack."

The sun dimmed suddenly, and both men looked skyward. A pall of smoke, gray and heavy in the early air, drifted north to south on the mild breeze, and the smell of burning grass filled the agency grounds with its pungent odor.

"What do you make of that, Sergeant?" Davis asked. "Do you think a homestead has been put to the torch?"

"Can't say for sure, sir. There is no soot or ash that I can see, so wherever the fire's coming from, it's burning fast and hot. The smoke is heavy, so whatever is burning must have some moisture to it."

"Yes," Davis agreed, nodding, "that's fairly close to the assessment I would have made. Thank you, Sergeant. Maybe I should send a patrol—"

"Beggin' the lieutenant's pardon, sir, and with all due respect, I think your first responsibility is here just now."

Remembering the warriors now turning and approaching the agency, Davis nodded curtly. "Deploy the troops in defensive position, Sergeant. Weapons at port arms, not to be aimed or fired until my command. The horses are to be held and ready to be brought up for pursuit. Are there any questions?"

"Yessir. Just one question, if you'll pardon my ignorance. I'm sure you meant to say, and I probably missed it, that you'd want a detachment inside the agency. That's what we're here mostly to protect."

"Of course, Sergeant. Detail half of Second Squad to defend the agency from within. I shouldn't have to point out the obvious to you."

"Yessir. Right away, sir."

Davis could feel the pressure building in his chest, and a sense of elation, mixed with dread, filled his mind. Combat was what he had volunteered to come West for. He was the last of a long line of military men produced by the Davis family, all officers and each distinguished in battle. He could not fail them, for he bore a legacy of pride, honor, and courage under fire.

But how could he be sure of his courage? It was all so different from what he had been taught at the Point, and from what he had heard as a boy, listening to the war tales of his grandfathers, uncles, and elder brothers. This was so confusing; there seemed to be no clear-cut rules to go by, and each decision was predicated upon the circumstances of the moment, not by standard military procedure as set forth in the book. And how would he fare when the lieutenant's bars and officer's status were of no protection? The enemy knew no concern for rank; if anything, he would be a greater prize as a result of his position than would be the men of lesser station.

A light film of perspiration formed on Davis' upper lip, in spite of the morning chill, and his shirt felt clammy on his back. He watched half of Second Squad run toward the agency office, holding Springfields at port arms. Their .45-caliber Schofield–Smith & Wessons bobbed in reversed holsters with their flaps cut away for easy access.

Already a long line of Indians had formed before the door, and Doug Collins was busily apportioning goods into brightly colored baskets, earthenware containers, and anything else that would hold the precious substances. When the four soldiers elbowed their way inside, Collins looked up from his work and there was instant anger in his eyes.

"What the hell do you think you're doing in here? Get out, goddammit! Can't you see I'm busier than a cat covering shit on a flat rock?"

Private Logan stopped, and the other three soldiers crowded up against him. "Lieutenant's orders, sir. We're supposed to help you defend the agency."

"From what?"

"Indians, sir."

"Indians! What the hell do you think these are," he asked hotly, his arm sweeping the air to indicate the crowded room. "Irishmen? They aren't. They're Indians, now get the hell out. If I need any protection, it's from you, not from them."

The Indians watched in silent confusion, wishing only to receive their rations, endure the humbling experience, and vanish back to their reserve as quickly as possible.

"Hey, Dink!" Logan called to the man nearest the door. "Go tell the sergeant that this feller don't want us in here."

The man named Dink ducked out the door and Collins went back to his work. Outside, the Arapaho bunched near the door began to mill around and move to one side as Eagle Flies Alone and his band rode directly into the heart of the crowd, riding slowly but with no intention of stopping their mounts should anyone refuse to move aside. There was a mixture of contempt and admiration on the faces of many of the elder tribesmen, a sense of longing for the old days, mixed with a dread of the consequences that the actions of these young braves might bring. It was surely Eagle Flies Alone's finest moment, and he sat proud and tall upon his pony, his blank, fathomless eyes staring ahead at the soldiers formed in an L-shaped firing line that crossed the street and ran at a right angle to the buildings on the near side.

When he pulled his pony to a stop, Eagle Flies Alone was but twenty yards from Lieutenant Davis, who stood before his troops and stared at the fierce-looking warrior. They matched stares in silence for nearly a full minute before the Indian turned his mount to face the crowd gathered behind him and watching the scene with a growing uneasiness. "Hear me, my people," his voice boomed in the stillness. "Take no more charity from the white man! He gives you these trinkets to make you forget all that he has taken. He has taken your land and your freedom, and now he is taking your pride! You stand there like children being punished for something you have not done. The old man, Gray Bear, talks of returning to the ways of our grandfathers before the white man came. But his are empty words, the words of a man who speaks no more with his lance and bow, but instead with hands held out in pleading. That is not the way to make things the way they were in the Grandfather times."

Eagle Flies Alone paused, using the closing silence as a weapon against his people and their thoughts of shame, and when he spoke again he brandished the heavy Spencer to the sky. "Heya, we must take what is ours! We must push the white settlers from our native land! We must show the blue-legs we have no fear of them!" He hesitated one last time. "We must make war! I have spoken!"

Lieutenant Davis, although nearly mesmerized by the warrior's speech, jolted forward with the last words and stepped quickly toward Eagle Flies Alone. He grasped the Indian's legging, and Eagle Flies Alone looked down in surprise from what had been his challenging stare at the assembled Arapaho.

"You, mister! Get down from that horse! You're under arrest by authority of the United States Army on the charge of participating in, and being a party to, acts in violation of the terms of agreement expressed in the treaty your people signed. I will not tolerate—"

The Indian's lip rolled into a curling sneer while the sudden thrust of his moccasin caught Davis full in the chest and sent him sprawling upon his back in the dust. The soldiers stirred restlessly behind them and some weapons were lifted, then reluctantly lowered upon a signal from Sergeant Olsen.

Eagle Flies Alone continued to stare at Davis, who was now scrambling to his knees. "You will not arrest anyone, blue-leg. And you will never again touch another Arapaho warrior. We do not care what you will tolerate. We are at war and you will be the first to die." He touched a moccasin to his pony's flank and moved into the crowd again, but this time the horse was pressed to a gallop and the Arapaho on foot scrambled for safety. There was mass confusion in the square before agency headquarters, and the high-pitched singsong of the Arapaho language only added to the confusion as Indians spilled from the building while others attempted to push their way in to profess their innocence of any involvement with the young firebrand.

Doug Collins, having been too preoccupied with his work to hear the renegade's words, was stunned by the sudden uproar, and he screamed above the noise and chatter for silence and order, neither of which were given.

"Sergeant Olsen!" Lieutenant Davis yelled, his face red, his cheeks quivering with rage. "Have the horses brought forward and have this unit mounted and ready to ride in sixty seconds. I want that heathen!"

The soldier named Dink hurried up to the sergeant's side. "Sergeant Olsen? The man don't want us inside his building. What'll we do?"

"You'll get your ass back in there and do as ordered! I didn't ask you to ask him if he liked it! He is using United States Government property, and protect it by God we will, until Lieutenant Kincaid gets back and tells us different. Now get your butt back in there and tell him that, and be prepared for an assault."

Dink hurried away, and Olsen turned again to the lieutenant. "Beggin' your pardon, sir, with all due respect to rank and all, but I think us chasin' them Injuns will likely get us two things: most of us killed in an ambush, and you—if you survive—a court-martial for losing your detachment and abandoning the property you were assigned to protect."

Davis watched Sergeant Olsen through glazed eyes, and the hatred and hurt slowly melted away and the real world came into focus once again. "No man can be allowed to treat an officer of the United States Army in a manner like that, Sergeant. He must be punished, and punished severely."

"And I'm sure you'll have an opportunity to do that, sir. But there is no need to chase him; he'll come to you. He's made his brag, now he has to back it up. Within the half-hour he will attack the agency, after he's had a chance to grease up."

"How do you know that, Sergeant?" Davis asked, a hint of genuine respect edging his voice.

"I've been here a long time, sir, I know the Indian mind. If you don't in this business, you're a dead man."

Davis glanced toward the now-vacant ridges and rolling hills.

"Within the half-hour, you say, Sergeant? Then tell the men to stay in their positions and—"

Sergeant Olsen ran a hand wearily through his hair, then replaced his hat against the increasing heat of the sun. "Beggin' your pardon, sir, with all—"

"Don't go through all the bullshit again, all right, Sergeant? Say what you have to say and I'll make a judgment as to its merit when you're through."

Olsen grinned, and his yellow teeth, discolored and worn through years of chewing plug tobacco, eating field rations, and drinking alkali water, caught the lieutenant's eye. He wondered how anyone could chew that vile stuff, much less enjoy it. Olsen spat, and the wad of brown juice ruffled the dust.

"That'll make it a might easier, sir, right enough," the sergeant said, squinting at the buildings situated within the walled compound. They were arranged in a square configuration around a central street, with an opening on either end serving as entrance and exit. "I think we'd be better off deploying our troops in the buildings and along the wall. We're here to protect property as well as lives, and if the Arapaho are still as fond of fire arrows as they used to be, things could get a mite hot around here before they cool off. I'm sure there ain't no water to spare, and nothin' to carry it in if there was, so we'll talk to old Doug and see how many blankets we can scare up. Use them to smother the flames if we got time. Better have the horses put in that stable over there, with a three-man guard posted on them. If Eagle Flies Alone is as serious as he seems to be, he'll try to drive the horses off first thing." Olsen spat again, then grinned once more. "I ain't got no intention of walkin' back to the outpost."

Davis nodded and there was a relieved look on his face. "You'll take care of the deployment of the troops and other little details like that then, Sergeant. I'd better talk with the agent and apprise him of our plans." He looked at the Indians, who were continuing to mill around the square and surge into and out of the agency building. "How about the rest of these people? Are they with us or against us?"

"Hard to tell. Depends mostly, I guess, on whose winnin' toward the end."

"That will be us, I'm certain."

Olsen worked a grimy finger into his cheek and lower lip, drew out a moist brown mess, and tossed it aside. "Custer thought the same thing, Lieutenant. Now he's a worm farm. Better see to the troops."

Davis watched the sergeant momentarily before turning toward the agency building. The Indians watched him curiously as he approached, and there was little respect in their eyes now that they'd seen him humiliated by Eagle Flies Alone. They gave way grudgingly as the lieutenant worked his way inside with polite expressions of apology. Collins looked up from his task briefly, then back down again.

"Mornin', Lieutenant. Some of your soldiers got lost and I been keepin' em' for ya," he said, inclining his head toward the rear of the building, where the four troopers, who had been lounging against the wall, lurched to their feet.

"Good morning, Mr. Collins. Those men are here to help with the protection of the agency."

"From what?"

"From the impending attack."

"By who?"

"Eagle Flies Alone and his braves. Didn't you hear his boastful remarks outside earlier?"

"Bullshit, horsefeathers, and poppycock. That kid's an overblown braggart who ain't got the brains God give a pissant."

"Then you don't think he will attack?"

"Not on your life."

Davis looked around the inside of the agency, and his eyes

found a staircase leading upward toward the rear of the building. "Do those steps go to the roof?"

Collins glanced up from measuring a ration of coffee into an old squaw's tightly woven basket. "They don't go to heaven. Why?"

"Mind if I put a couple of my men on the roof? Just as a precaution?"

"Your men, government's building. Put 'em wherever in hell you want to."

"Thank you, Mr. Collins. And I'll be needing whatever spare blankets you have, as well."

"What there are will be back in the storeroom. Help yourself, but bring 'em back." He winked at the lieutenant before bending again to his work. "Boys gonna have a little nap, are they, Lieutenant?"

"No. They are going to save your life and keep your agency in one piece. At least you'd better hope they do."

"No shit?"

"Believe it, Mr. Collins. Believe it."

Outside, the remainder of the platoon was scrambling into position; the men were climbing onto rooftops and barricading themselves behind the doors of shops and trade buildings. There were sixteen troopers; counting Davis and Olsen, eighteen men of Easy Company were preparing to defend against sixty Arapaho, plus who knew how many among those now milling about the compound that might join in the fray. Olsen instructed his men not to fire upon anyone other than the braves who had joined with Eagle Flies Alone, but to watch the others just in case they got carried away.

There was a weird, almost surrealistic air about the agency compound as they waited for Eagle Flies Alone to press the attack. Within the square, the peaceful Arapaho continued to mill about. Those who had obtained their rations slowly trudged away from the agency, and those who had not were standing before the building and waiting, amid the restless chatter, for their turns. Atop the buildings and behind heavy doors, the blue-clad soldiers waited for death to come, whether by bullet or by bow, and they were silent as they watched the shimmering plains in the heat of the late-morning sun.

It began without warning. One moment the rise three hundred yards west of the compound was nothing but a tranquil scene of tall grass waving in the increasing breeze, devoid of life, man or beast. And the next moment, barechested, bronzed warriors, masked in grotesque stripings of green and bent low over ponies running full speed across the plains, burst over the gentle ridge, and their shouts and screams were carried to the compound on the wind. The Indians in the square began to run for their mounts or seek shelter beside the buildings. When the first pony, with a green circle around its left eye, burst through the main gate, ridden by Eagle Flies Alone, they scattered. One young boy fell beneath the horse's hooves.

Paying no attention to the victim, the warrior pulled his stumbling mount's head up and pressed it to a full run once again, while rolling off to the left side of his pony, aiming the Spencer beneath his horse's neck, and firing on the agency as he raced by. Two shots thundered into the wall behind Collins' back; the third slammed into the iron stove in the corner with a crashing ring, and the stovepipe collapsed in a spray of soot.

Behind Eagle Flies Alone, thirty more warriors thundered through the compound, firing rifles and arrows indiscriminately. Two more Indians went down, one a young woman and the other an old man, and a trooper tumbled from a rooftop and crashed facedown in the dust. Blood pouring from his chest formed a thick, muddy pool beneath his face.

The return fire from the rooftops and doorways was intense, and four riderless Indian ponies galloped away from the compound, while a fifth horse, having been dragged down by its dead rider, hobbled around the square on a broken leg with white bone protruding and glistening with blood.

The fire arrows were quick to follow, and even the uninitiated could see that the initial raid had been used as a screen to get the marksmen close enough to fire at their targets without being seen. The arrows, usually traveling on a fast, low trajectory, now lobbed into the compound with their rag-and-pitch-laden tips trailing ugly black smoke and striking rooftops, doorways, or anything wooden that might catch fire immediately.

Doug Collins was shocked beyond words, and when Lieutenant Davis sprinted down the staircase from the roof, he saw the agent staring at his stove in disbelief.

"What the hell's going on here?" Collins asked, looking first at the bewildered Indians milling around the room and then at the officer.

A fire arrow sailed heavily through the window and thudded,

sizzling, against the far wall. Davis sprang forward, seized the arrow, and stamped it out while another burning missile glanced off the open door and struck a young Indian squarely in the back. He screamed and fell to the floor, writhing in pain as fire quickly enveloped the back of his shirt.

"What the hell's going on here?" Collins yelled again, incredulous and unable to comprehend what was happening. The Indians standing outside continued to push their way inside, and one pulled the arrow from the young man's back and smothered the flames consuming his shirt. Those inside the building surged around Collins and loudly professed their innocence of any involvement in the uprising. Another arrow sailed through the door as yet another stuck in the window ledge, where its flames quickly found dry wood, while two more slammed into the back wall.

"Close that damned door and shutter the window," Davis screamed, trying to press through the mass of bodies and failing. He could hear riflefire coming from the street, as well as much screaming and yelling, and he felt a sense of pride at his own calmness and grasp of the deteriorating situation.

Flames blackened the back wall and Collins, finally breaking clear of his semi-trance, fought to escape the excited, jabbering Arapaho surrounding him and extinguish the flames. When Davis could see that the agent was again in control of his senses, he yelled over the general din, "Get that door and window closed! I've got to get back to the roof and make sure we're not going to be rushed."

Bounding up the stairs again, Davis sprang through the trapdoor and ran at a crouch to the edge of the building, where the four soldiers continued their systematic firing. Some of the braves had dismounted now, and were infiltrating the compound and taking refuge in vacant buildings and behind wagons or any other cover available. Two buildings burned out of control, and the blackish-gray smoke rose on intense heat and mingled with the haze darkening the sky.

Counting the soldiers he could see on the rooftops and those he could see firing from windows and doorways, Davis realized that two of his soldiers were dead, and his eyes went to the four warpainted braves lying in the street. The anger that swept over him was nearly uncontrollable. He pulled the Scoff from his holster, dropped to his stomach, and fired four quick rounds at fleeting buckskin darting from one building to the next. A bullet slammed into the log structure before him from the opposite direction, and Davis fired his remaining two rounds blindly at the new target before slumping down, turning on his back, and jamming six fresh shells into the pistol.

Concentrating on his work, with sweat seeping down his forehead and into his eyes, Davis had just snapped the cylinder shut and glanced up as a young brave, with bizarre green and white markings trailing from his eyes to his lower jaw, clambered onto the roof from the back of the building. Davis and the Arapaho were each equally startled by the other's presence, and they stared at each other for what seemed an eternity while the four soldiers continued to fire, oblivious to the warrior behind them.

The Indian's rifle was coming up, and Davis raised the revolver from his lap. With what felt to him like agonizing slowness, he pulled the trigger and the heavy shell smacked into the young brave's lower chest, lifting him with a startled look from the rooftop and slamming him against the breastwork of the building. The rifle clattered from his hands, and as he lay there, a wheezing sigh escaped his chest and caused the blood to bubble from the hole torn in his bare skin.

Davis watched the warrior in silence for several seconds before lifting the revolver and staring at it as though he were shocked to have the weapon in his hand. His eyes went back to the warrior, perhaps even younger than Davis himself, and he felt a momentary twinge of remorse. He had killed his first man.

Sergeant Olsen burst through the trapdoor, located the lieutenant, than ran toward him, crouched low against incoming fire. He knelt beside the officer and watched the blank-eyed man staring at the silent form across from him. Olsen glanced once at the warrior, then back to Davis.

"Sir," Olsen said, shaking Davis' arm, "he ain't gonna get any deader, no matter how long you sit there and stare at him."

Davis stirred and his gaze went to the sergeant. "Huh? What?"

"You killed a man, sir. Congratulations. About thirty more just like that, and we'll be out of the mess we're in."

"Mess, Sergeant?" Davis asked, his eyes clearing now and stirring to life. "What mess? We're holding them, aren't we?"

"We have been, sir, but I don't know for how much longer. We've lost three men, several buildings are on fire, and I think we might have to fort up here in the agency. The Araps are infiltrating the compound with what I figure, adding in the jolly lads with the fire arrows who are now joining the attack, to be two-thirds of their braves. That leaves fifteen or so still being held back. Some of them featherheads are armed with Spencer repeaters, which gives them a real edge over us, with our single-shot Springfields. Twenty men firing repeaters is about the same as forty with breech-loaders." The sergeant spat toward the dead warrior and tobacco splashed beside his head. "Fortunately, most of these simpleminded bastards couldn't hit the broad side of a barn from the inside or we'd be finished already."

"Where would they get Spencers, Sergeant, when we haven't even been issued them?"

Olsen glanced over the breastwork, then back to Davis. "Beats the shit out of me, and right now I don't really give a fuck. They got 'em, that's all that matters. We're gonna need some covering fire to get First Squad out of those buildings across the street and over on this side. Have these lads—" Olsen swung a hand toward the street to indicate his intentions, but the hand stopped, pointing toward the north, and Olsen frowned.

Turning, Davis squinted in the direction indicated by the sergeant. "Now who the hell is that?"

"Good question, sir. Very good question," Olsen said.

They fell silent and watched the eight riders streaking toward the compound and firing at the band of braves who suddenly materialized over the low swale and were riding hard at an oblique angle to cut them off. Leather chaps slapping against legs were visible now, and wide-brimmed Stetsons were bent back against the wind.

"It's those cowhands, sir," Olsen offered. "At least I think it is."

Davis watched several seconds longer. "You're right, Sergeant. What the hell are they doing here?"

"Even though they may not know it, sir, they might be savin' our bacon. Looks like they're gonna beat them drum-thumpers to the compound, and with eight more rifles. What with those eight being Winchesters, we can hold this agency till Lieutenant Kincaid gets back."

"That's a bit ignominious, isn't it, Sergeant? An army unit being saved by civilians?"

"Igno . . . what?"

"Ignominious."

"I don't know about that, and I ain't much used to them ten-dollar words. But I will tell you what's 'igno' for sure. It's damned igno*rant* to give a fuck who saves your ass, long as they get it saved." Olsen crouched beside the four troopers lying against the log on the edge of the roof. "Come on, lay it to that building across the way. Those cowboys don't know they got hostiles to contend with, once they get inside the compound."

Rising and exposing himself to Indian weapons, Olsen signaled for the other men of Easy Company to concentrate their fire on the doorways and windows of the buildings the infiltrating Indians had occupied. Using the advantage of superior elevation, they continued to lay down a withering field of riflefire even as the cowboys pounded into the compound and leaped from their sliding mounts.

One brave rose up and snapped off a quick shot before a .40-caliber slug, powered by eighty-five grains of black powder, smashed into his throat and threw him spinning against the wall, to sag lifeless there. The cowhands, seeing the presence of the enemy behind them, crouched behind whatever cover they could find and joined in the heavy barrage of lead raining into the buildings. The remaining Indians slipped through back doorways and windows to melt away on the plains as quickly as they had come.

Before the gate, which sagged uselessly on broken hinges, Eagle Flies Alone and his mounted braves stopped just out of rifle range and watched the compound silently for several minutes before they turned and disappeared over the crest of a rolling rise.

The silence inside the compound was crushing in the sudden absence of noise. Where rifle shots and screamed shouts had boomed in echoing reverberations, now there was only the sharp crackling of flames consuming dry wood.

Lieutenant Davis struggled to his feet and straightened his uniform with several sharp tugs. "Not exactly a textbook defense," he said, stooping to retrieve his hat, "but it looks like we repulsed them."

"Yeah, for now, sir. But I'll tell you one thing, Lieutenant. That Eagle Flies Alone feller means business. Lieutenant Kincaid don't know nothin' about this. Kind of easy to ambush a man who thinks there's a peace goin' on. Hope to hell they're stayin' on their toes."

"Mandalian and he seem pretty capable of taking care of themselves," Davis said, his tone not entirely confident.

"Two of the best in the business," Olsen said, nodding in agreement. "But there's still places where even the best can't avoid an ambush. If anybody knows those places, it's gotta be these sneaky, snake-eyed Arapaho. They came after us, ain't no reason why they won't try to take out the lieutenant."

"When do you expect him back?"

"When I see his horse come over the rise. Come on. I think we'd better check out the troops."

six

"Hey, Sergeant? Mind coming in here a second?" Captain Conway asked, laying the dispatch from regimental headquarters aside and leaning back in his chair. There was a tranquility about the midmorning stillness that he liked, and if only the top brass could pull themselves together just once, he felt he could even enjoy the day.

First Sergeant Ben Cohen hesitated in the office doorway before stepping inside. "You called me, sir?"

"Yes I did. Have a seat."

The captain selected a long, thin cigar from a wooden box and shoved the container across as Cohen sat down. "Care for one?" he asked while moistening the cigar between his lips and digging a match from his desk drawer.

"Thank you, sir," Cohen responded, and selected a cigar from the fragrant box.

Conway struck the match and smelled the heavy fumes of sulfur as he let the head burn away before touching the flame to the tips of both cigars, first Cohen's and then his own. Then both men leaned back comfortably and puffed their cigars to life, releasing odorous swirls of blue smoke. Finally, Captain Conway glanced up and said, "You ever wonder what makes us do it, Sergeant?"

"Do what, sir?"

"Put up with all this bullshit?"

"No more than fifty minutes of every waking hour of the day, sir," Cohen replied with a smile.

Conway nodded. "That's about right. Here we are, pulling the worst duty the army has to offer; nearly everyone to a man is overage in grade, including you, Matt, myself, everybody; we can't get the supplies we need, we should be armed with Spencers instead of Springfields; and now, as usual, the payroll is five days late. You'd think, for Christ's sake, they'd at least keep us paid in the hope of keeping us quiet, wouldn't you?"

"Yeah, that makes it tough on everybody. We have enough

morale problems around here as it is, without throwin' in no pay on payday." Cohen flicked an ash into the tray on the captain's desk as he said, "Word has it in the sewing circles that a lot of wives are encouraging their men to quit the military because of the foolishness that's going on back at regiment."

"Sewing circles, Sergeant?" Conway asked, grinning around the cigar clamped between his front teeth. "I guess I wasn't aware of your off-duty pleasures."

The tough old sergeant might have reddened, but his skin was too bronzed to tell. "It ain't my pleasure, sir. But Maggie does a bit of it, and bein' quiet about what she hears, and especially what she thinks, is not one of her strong suits."

Conway laughed as he thought about Maggie Cohen, perhaps one of the finest service wives he had known. Strong, courteous, always available when needed, never complaining, always serving and behind her man one hundred percent. She was the guiding pillar for the enlisted men's wives and was devoted to the captain's own wife, Flora. Maggie Cohen was not a beautiful woman externally, but she possessed the soul of a saint and the Irish temper of a rapparee when riled. And Captain Conway thought the world of her.

"Maggie's a sweetheart, Ben. There aren't many women like her in the service."

Cohen grinned. "And there are many who would count that as a blessing, Captain."

"Bullshit and jealousy, that's all, Ben." Conway's eyes turned serious and he puffed the cigar in momentary silence. "No dispatches have come in from Lieutenant Kincaid yet, eh?"

"Nossir. Been gone three days now, but that's not unusual. Are you concerned, sir?"

"I'm always concerned with a unit in the field, you know that. But yes, I am a little more concerned than usual. Just a sort of nagging hunch, know what I mean?"

"Yessir. I thrive on 'em."

"I'll bet you do. Anyway, I've got one of those hunches about this patrol. Something just doesn't seem right about it. Maybe a platoon wasn't a large enough force to handle whatever in hell could have gone wrong."

"If you'll pardon my sayin' so, sir, that kind of thinkin' is like throwin' slop water into the wind, ain't it? With the lieutenant and Windy together, I'd hate to be the Arapaho who fucked up, and if I was a soldier ridin' behind 'em I'd feel safer than a baby suckin' on its momma's tit. Whatever happens will happen, and we can't worry about it till it does."

"You're right, Ben. Absolutely correct." The captain winked at the man across from him. "Still, I plan to sneak in a worry now and then."

"That'll make two of us, then," the sergeant returned with a knowing grin.

"When Matt does get back, I'm going to ride into Regiment and raise just a touch of hell about this pay business. Every month's the same damned thing and I'm tired of it. I'll not see my men mishandled by some dumb paymaster sitting on his fat ass at headquarters and playing God with the future of my troops."

"That's good, sir, I think you should. If for no other reason than to get some of it off your chest. Everybody else has got somebody to bitch at around here except you. I think Regiment's overdue for a word from Captain Conway."

"And that they'll get. Since everything else goes wrong around here, I might just as well put *my* foot in the shit, too."

Sergeant Cohen pushed his chair away with his legs and started to rise. "Well, there is one bright spot, sir, and it's to be found in the least likely place imaginable."

"Really? Tell me about it."

"You issued a three-day pass to Private Malone yesterday, remember?"

"I remember, and it was against my better judgment, I might add. Go ahead."

"He spent a whole night in town and part of another day, and as far as I know he's not in jail and he hasn't been brought back here by the military police. That makes damned near thirty-six hours. A record for Malone, I think."

"Damned if you're not right," Conway said with a chuckle. "That is something of a record, I'm sure. How the hell did he ever have enough money to go to town, with this being two days after payday and no pay?"

"You've had him restricted since before last payday, sir. Because of that latest fight with the feather merchants, as he calls the businessmen in town. He asked me to hold his pay until he got a pass, so when you gave him that pass, I gave him his money." Cohen shook his head and turned toward the doorway. "Damned strange thing about Malone. He'd be one damned fine soldier if the army would do just one thing."

"What's that, Ben?"

"Quit payin' the son of a bitch!"

Conway laughed and stubbed the cigar out in the ashtray. "You've got a point there, Sarge. Too bad it won't work. I tried something different this time, though, before he left. Maybe it's working. I told him to stay away from that laundry woman of his. What's her name?"

"Rosemarie O'Conner."

"Yeah, that's it. They get drunk together, then get to fighting between themselves. Malone gets pissed off at her and goes into town like a one-eyed, blood-mad stud bull on the rampage, and Lord help the civilian that crosses him. Maybe for once he listened to my advice."

Sergeant Cohen turned in the doorway with an apologetic grin on his face. "You told him to stay away from Rosemarie, Captain? Was that a direct order?"

"No. Just sort of father-to-son, heart-to-heart, as it were."

"Then good luck to you and your advice, sir. Asking Malone to stay away from Rosemarie is like telling a rooster not to crow at the rising sun. He ain't gonna listen to ya, even if he could."

"Ah, Rosemarie, me heart, you'd be truly the one thing of beauty in this barren land. And there'd not be a rose in all of Killarney that'd match your smile, to be tellin' the truth now."

Private Malone was proud of his poetic observation as he took up his whiskey glass to contemplate further metaphors and admire the slightly thick-bodied, totally naked, and somewhat pretty woman by his side.

Rosemarie smiled and, snatching the covers, pulled them to her chin in one hasty motion, saying, "And there'd not be a man in all of Ireland who'd be needin' to kiss the Blarney Stone more than yourself, Mr. Malone."

"*Mr.* Malone is it, now?" Private Malone asked in mock surprise. "Would you be expectin' me to call you *Miss* O'Conner in return of kindness?"

They looked at each other with grinning eyes, and Rosemarie reached over and gently took the glass of rye whiskey from Malone's hand, while the other slipped beneath the covers to caress his inner thigh. "Call me whatever you'd be wantin' to call me, love, but don't call me late for supper."

A smile creased Malone's face and he hoisted his wide,

muscular body up against the headboard of the bed. He crossed his thick forearms over a massive chest and the biceps bulged as he watched Rosemarie drink generously from the glass. Her hand moved upward and Malone's voice became husky.

"Keep that up, love, and you're gonna be late for everthin' you'd planned to do today."

Rosemarie watched him with a coquettish grin. "Am I?" she asked, teasing the rim of the glass with her tongue. "Tell me about it."

"Might I be havin' a drink of me own whiskey?"

Rosemarie watched him momentarily, then leaned over and held the glass to his lips. The covers fell away and her large, firm breasts pressed against Malone's arm as she tilted the glass. Malone remained motionless, save for opening his mouth and swallowing, even when the whiskey trickled from the corners of his mouth and dripped onto his chest. Pulling the glass away, she kissed him, gently at first and then with increasing passion, and when their lips parted, she worked her mouth first to his ear, then to his neck, and down to his chest. With just the tip of her tongue, she began to lick and suck the whiskey from his smooth skin, and her breathing was coming more sharply, in concert with the irregular heaving of Malone's chest.

Malone gently took the glass from her hand as she worked toward his stomach, taut, firm, and flat but sensitive and tensed. Her tongue touched his navel, circled it several times, then continued downward, across the tender lower stomach region to gently caress the upper inner thigh. Malone could contain himself no longer, and he squirmed involuntarily, wishing for her lips and straining to find them, a bull of a man with but one blinding, white-hot thought searing his mind while his huge hands went gently to the back of her head and buried themselves in reddish-brown hair. With great patience and infinite skill, Rosemarie worked her man to a fever pitch, and finally her mouth closed over him in a flood of softness and warmth.

And then the pounding came upon the door.

Malone's eyes snapped open and the ecstatic groaning ceased to escape his lips. Rosemarie looked up, still holding him in her mouth, with a startled, questioning look in her eyes. The pounding came again and there was a demanding impatience to the sound.

"Who the hell'd that be, Rosemarie?" Malone hissed.

Rosemarie pulled away and Malone reluctantly freed her head of his hands. "I have no idea, love. Be quiet as a little church mouse now, and maybe they'll go on like they should," she said, her mouth lowering toward him again as another pounding rattled the doorjamb.

Malone pushed her away. "They'll not be leavin, lass, I'm as certain of that as of tomorrow's shit detail," he said, his voice just above a whisper. "Maybe I'd better put on me clothes and see who it is."

Rosemarie sat up quickly and adjusted her hair while scooting to the edge of the bed. Malone thought he saw a strange concern in her eyes.

"No, love, you stay right here, it has to be a mistake. Who would be knockin' on my door this time of day? I'll see who it is and send them on their way." She pulled on a robe, tightened the sash around her waist, and adjusted the material over her bulging breasts, then paused to lean down and kiss Malone on the cheek as she whispered, "Stay right here and don't forget where we were."

Malone smiled and shook his head. "How could I forget?"

The renewed pounding was louder than before, and a deep voice rose above the thunder. "Rosemarie? I know you're in there! It's Benjy, just come home to see momma! Let me in, you beautiful little wench, I been a long time in the bull pasture!"

The smile faded from Malone's lips at the same rate that the concern deepened in Rosemarie's eyes. "Now don't be thinkin' what you're thinkin' . . ." she began with a falter in her voice.

"And what would I be thinkin', other than that whoever the hell's out there ain't made no mistake, and who the fuck is Benjy?" Malone said with little concern for volume.

"Sssshhhhhhh!" Rosemarie implored with a finger pressed against her full lips. "He's an old friend who comes by the laundry now and then."

"To get his ashes hauled?" Malone said, the demanding tone in his voice rising to match the pounding on the door. "I wasn't knowin' you was in that business too, and for the whole damned town yet."

"Now you hold onto your britches, Mr. Malone . . ."

"I ain't got none to hold onto, but I damned well will have, as soon as I can find 'em. What the hell did you do with me trousers?"

"They're on the chair, damn you! Don't be accusin' me of somethin' you'd do yourself if you had the chance . . ."

"With Benjy? Not on your life," Malone said dragging on his pants and reaching for his socks and boots.

"I didn't mean with him, dammit, and you'd be knowin' that as well as me. Besides, you've been restricted to that damned post for over a month now. A girl gets a little lonely and—"

"I ain't exactly been tangled up with no harems meself, lass, and you'd better tell Benjy that if he touches that fucking door one more time, he'll be wearin' it for a hatband!"

Malone was stomping into his boots now, and Rosemarie glanced furtively toward the door. "Benjy! Stop that foolishness now and go away! I'll talk to you later."

There was silence while Malone pulled on his tunic, draped the light blue neckerchief across his shoulders, and perched the gray campaign hat with its crossed rifles on his head.

"Is that you in there, Rosemarie?" the voice outside the door asked.

"No, ya bleedin' idiot," Malone replied, tightening the buckle on the gunbelt that held the twin, reversed-position revolvers around his waist, "it's the Midnight Maiden from Mercy Street!"

"Malone! You big jackass!" Rosemarie yelled, swinging at him but missing.

"Who the hell is in there? Open this door before I break it down!"

"It's openin' right now, bucko, and all that I'd be wantin' to see on the other side is air." Malone turned with one hand on the knob and grinned at Rosemarie while his other hand went out to pat her rump. "Keep the gates to hell closed for me till I get back, will you, love? Probably be another month."

"Malone? Don't go doin' nothin' foolish now, ya hear me?"

"Foolish? I already did that. Now I'm just gonna have a little fun."

Malone threw the door aside and the startled man, with his hand raised to knock again, stepped backward. He was every bit of six foot four, approximating Malone's height, and he was built with equal brawn. The black felt hat and flannel shirt, as well as the jeans tucked into high black boots, labeled him as a teamster, and the mocking look in his eyes as they roamed up and down Malone indicated that he didn't frighten easily.

"Well, if it ain't a soldier boy! Rosemarie, you'll be havin' to take a good hot bath to get some of that cavalry stink off of ya before I can love ya right and proper."

"Benjy, don't—"

Rosemarie's words were wasted as Malone's fist shot out and slammed full force against the teamster's chin, followed by a wicked left to the solar plexus. Benjy doubled at the waist and Malone's knee met his head as it came down. Benjy's head snapped back, his broad shoulders crashed against the wall, and he slumped slowly to the floor.

Malone paused over the unconscious form, dug a coin from his pocket, and dropped it on the man's chest. "Tell the lad there when he wakes up that I'm mounted infantry, not cavalry. Them kind of mistakes could get him killed, not to mention keepin' time with the wrong man's woman. And tell him I'll be down at the Drover's Rest wettin' me whistle if he'd like to pursue this matter a wee bit further." He winked at Rosemarie while rubbing his bruised knuckles. "You're a beauty, lass. At least the man's got good taste, if nothin' else."

Malone moved down the street with long, ground-eating strides, and stepped onto the boardwalk in front of the saloon with a solid thump of his boots. Hesitating for a second, he let his hand rest on the batwing doors and listened to the familiar sounds of men drinking, laughing, and talking. Then he stepped inside and approached the bar.

"What'll it be?" The bartender asked amicably.

"Whiskey. Make it a double and leave the bottle."

The bartender nodded, poured the drink, collected his money, then aimlessly began to polish the bar with sweeping, circular motions of a white towel.

"How's things goin'?" he asked, obviously trying to make conversation.

Malone downed his drink and poured another. "Could be worse. Could be better."

The man behind the bar nodded. "Been in the army long?"

"Too long."

"Cavalry?"

Malone looked at the bartender for the first time. "Mounted infantry."

"What the hell's that? Either you walk or you ride, one or the other."

"We do both."

"Seems strange to me . . ."

"Look, mister, I've got some things on me mind that makes drinkin' alone a pleasure. If you don't mind, I'll take up what I come in here to do, and that's get drunk alone, real quiet and peaceful-like."

The bartender, a fairly young man with a hint of Eastern accent, was either hurt or angered by Malone's remark and gave the bar a final, vicious swipe. "Sure, fella, I'm kinda new around here and was just tryin' to make conversation."

"I noticed that," Malone said as the bartender moved away. He didn't look up or acknowledge the man's departure, and stood there slowly turning the glass in his fingertips.

An older man farther down the bar had been listening to the attempted conversation, and watched the bartender approach. "Don't pay any attention to them army fellas, son. They think they own the world just 'cause they wear a uniform and carry a gun. And we pay their wages on top of it all."

The muscles bulged at the corners of Malone's jaw, but he remained silent, downing the glass before him and splashing in a refill.

"Well, he's sure as hell got an attitude problem, that's—" The bartender stopped talking and his eyes jerked toward the twin batwings, which slammed apart with a sound of splintering wood.

Malone's eyes went once to the mirror behind the bar, then back to his drink.

"There ya are, ya sucker-punchin' son of a bitch!" The teamster, Benjy, stood in the doorway with arms akimbo and hatred blazing in his eyes. "Seems to me it's time for one bluebelly to learn respect for his betters, and that it ain't healthy to sneak around trying to take advantage of another man's woman."

"Fuck off, mate," Malone said, without turning around.

Benjy crossed the room in three strides and slammed a punch against the side of Malone's head, just above the right ear. The gray campaign hat tilted forward as Malone swung an elbow and caught the teamster in the solar plexus. Benjy swung another blow that missed, then was rocked backward by two quick left jabs and a crossing right.

Malone was now concentrating on the task before him, and a wild, almost trancelike glint had come into his eyes. He hadn't seen the short, stocky man follow Benjy into the saloon and he nearly went to his knees as a chair crashed upon the broad of his back and disintegrated into kindling. In one motion, Malone spun, grabbed the man by the shirtfront and crotch, hoisted him into the air, and hurled him onto the nearest table to send drinks, bottles, and poker chips rolling and skidding across the floor. Then Malone turned back to work on Benjy, who had gotten to his knees and was now lunging forward with a bearlike leap and a gargling scream in his throat.

The element of surprise having been eliminated for both men, they were quite evenly matched. Nearly five minutes had passed by the time Malone threw one tremendous punch that sent the teamster back-pedaling across the room to crash, butt-first, through the front window and sprawl unconscious upon the boardwalk. The sheriff lumbered down the street while Malone wiped a trickle of blood from the corner of his mouth, carefully retrieved the campaign hat from the floor, adjusted its creases with maximum care, then stepped up to the bar, propped a boot on the foot rail, and drank a long pull straight from the bottle. Behind him the room was a complete shambles, with tables and chairs overturned or broken. Shattered bottles and glasses littered the room, and the townsmen slowly moved away from the shelter of doorways and window ledges to search for possessions strewn about in the fight.

The bartender eased along the bar and nervously twisted the towel in his hands as though it might provide some protection. "Look, soldier, I think you'd better—"

"I didn't start it," Malone said without looking up.

"Well, you didn't try to stop it."

Now the Irishman looked up. "No, I didn't try, bucko. I *did* stop it."

The sheriff, a heavyset elderly man, heaved up against the doorway, panted several quick breaths, then moved into the saloon. He saw the broad shoulders of the towering man drinking silently by himself, and he slammed his palm down upon the bar.

"Goddammit, Malone!"

The soldier turned and an easy grin spread across his face. "May I be wishin' a good day to you, sheriff?"

"Good day, my ass! What's the meaning of this?"

"Meanin', sir?" Malone glanced around innocently. "The place is a bit of a mess for gentlemen to drink in, but we'll get by, I suppose."

"There won't be any 'we' as far as you're concerned, Malone. Who started his donnybrook?"

"The lad sleepin' by the window outside seemed to throw the first punch. I wasn't countin' much after that, except that the feller over there"—Malone pointed to the man crawling dazedly out from under a table—"seems to have a terrible dislike for chairs. I was totally innocent of any provocation."

"Sure you were, Malone. As usual. And as usual, I want your ass out of town just as fast as I can get the regimental MPs here to haul you away."

Malone smiled again. "Would you be havin' a wee bit of a drink with me, sheriff, just while we're waitin'? Gets mighty thirsty in the guardhouse back at the post."

The sheriff hesitated, undecided, before finally waving to the bartender to set up two drinks. Despite all the fights the big Irishman inevitably became involved in, the sheriff still liked him and admired him for his combat record. And he also knew that if ever he were out of aces and the chips were down, the amicable Irishman would back him in anything that was decent and fair. Private Malone seemed to be one of those people who would always be involved in some sort of ridiculous situation, most of them usually not of his making, and while the sheriff contemplated his drink, he turned to Malone.

"How is it that you always wind up with your ass in a sling, Malone? You seem like a damned good soldier and a hell of a man, but I have to keep lockin' you up or runnin' you off ever' damned time you manage to sneak your way into town. Wouldn't it be better if that situation was different?"

A bemused, almost quizzical look came into Malone's eyes. "There's an old sayin' that I been kinda steerin' my life by, sheriff. 'Wish in one hand and shit in the other, and see which gets full the fastest.' Wishin' things was different don't buy no whiskey." Malone downed his drink and pushed away from the bar. "Shall we get this over with, constable?"

Sergeant Cohen watched the man who was standing before him so stiffly at attention that the arched back caused his chest to bulge threateningly against the buttons on his tunic. He stood frozen in position; an occasional gust of wind tugged at his scarf and provided the only vestige of life. He noticed the dark blue swell under the man's right eye, the puffed lips in the corner of his mouth, and the skin broken and raw across his knuckles.

Cohen, his hands crossed behind his back, walked slowly back and forth before the massive soldier. "Malone," he said finally, "there is no way known to me that I can restrict you to this post forever. If I ever find that regulation, please rest assured I'll use it at the first opportunity. Which will, I'm certain, be immediately after your next visit to town. If there was any way I could refuse to pay you for the remainder of your tour here, that I would do as well. But since I can't, I guess we'll just have to muck along the way we are."

"If the sergeant will pardon me sayin' so, the army's doin' a pretty good job on that themselves."

Cohen stopped his pacing and turned toward Malone. "What do you mean by that, Malone?"

"Mucking along when it comes to payin' the troops."

Cohen resisted the temptation to smile. "Yes, it appears they are. But we're not standing here to discuss the army, are we, Private? We are here to discuss you. When will you accept the fact that you cannot, I repeat, *cannot* possibly whip every feather merchant west of the Mississippi? And I say that with ultimate confidence from a strictly logistical point of view, if nothin' else."

"Why's that, Sarge?"

"Because you can't get your hands on every goddamned one of them, that's why!"

Malone smiled and a trickle of blood seeped from the fresh crack in his split lips. "Sure is a pleasure when I do get one, though, I'll tell you that for a fact."

"Obviously," Cohen said, turning and taking his right hand from behind his back. In it he held two tablespoons commandeered from the mess hall. He held the spoons up for Malone to see.

"Do you, in your infinite ignorance, have any idea what these are?"

Malone's eyes shifted to the sergeant's hand, then back to stare at the horizon. "Sort of look like spoons, Sarge."

"Sort of look like spoons," Cohen echoed in a mocking tone. "You know goddamned well they're spoons! But I'll bet you don't know what makes these spoons special."

"They ain't got no egg on 'em?"

"You're priceless, Malone, you really are. And to think others, just like you, came—and are coming—over here by the boatload. But, egg or no egg, that's not what makes these spoons so special. What makes them special is the fact that you are going to dig a six-by-six outside the walls with them. Now, you can dig with them two at a time, one at a time, rotate, alternate, I don't give a fuck, but you are gonna dig. Have you got that, Private Malone?"

"I think so, Sarge. You've made it fairly clear. When do I start?"

"Right now, this second, this day in the year of Our Lord, 1877. I want it exactly six foot on a side and six foot deep. And with each scoop I want you to say to yourself, 'I'll never touch another feather merchant as long as I live.'"

"Do I have to say that out loud?"

"No. I just want you to think it." Cohen handed the spoons across. "Here's your tools. Get with it."

"I'll think about them feather merchants while I'm diggin' there in the sun, Sarge," Malone said, grinning again. "You bet, I'll be thinkin' a whole lot about 'em."

seven

The afternoon shadows were lengthening rapidly as Matt, Windy, and the Third Squad of Easy Company worked their way down from the high country. The going was easy, the grass plentiful; the tranquility of the parklike setting in the cool of the mountain had a lulling effect on what would otherwise have been a constant vigilance.

There was hardly any sound except the occasional screech of a bird searching for its mate, the sharp chatter of a squirrel upset about something in a world he knew to be his, the soft jangle of rifles swaying in saddle spiders, and the swishing squeak of horses' hooves and legs threading a trail through the tall grass.

In the distance, out of sight and hidden below a steep cliff, the Little Feather River flowed with a hushed gurgling as it meandered toward the plains. The meadow through which they were riding was captured in an old glacial bowl carved in the earth's crust millions of years before and bordered on two sides by sharp crests of ragged stone, impassable on horseback.

Where the meadow met the river, there was a narrow trail, possibly two hundred yards in length and no more than four feet in width at the widest places, which led down to a second meadow breasting the prairie. At the bottom, where the trail ended and the meadow began, three tall alder trees laid claim to the riverbank along a sandy stretch of beach. Where the trail went down, water through the centuries had coursed and worked to carve small caverns and indentations into the sides of the cliff.

When they reached the mouth of the trail, Kincaid signaled for the column to halt and they allowed their horses to snatch delicious mouthfuls of grass while the soldiers relaxed in their saddles and basked in the peace and beauty of nature's offering.

"This is what the Arapaho call Three Trees, isn't it, Windy?" Matt asked as he looked down at the dark pools where a series of waterfalls spilled water from one to the next lower.

There was a wary look on the scout's face while he shifted in the saddle and studied the surrounding terrain with cautious eyes. "Yup. It is for a fact," he replied in a distant voice, as though his thoughts were elsewhere. "Perfect place for an ambush if anyone was so inclined."

"That's what I was thinking. Is there any way around it?"

"Nope. Not unless you want to backtrack upriver about ten miles."

"We haven't got time for that."

"I know. So, welcome to Three Trees."

Suddenly, Windy held his hand upward for silence. All ears strained to pick up what the scout might have heard, but it was not an alien sound that brought the concerned look to Mandalian's face—it was a peculiar odor perceived only by him.

Nearly two minutes went by before Matt leaned closer to the scout and asked in a voice just above a whisper, "What's troubling you, Windy?"

"Can't tell for certain, Matt, but I think that breeze is carryin' a trace of bear grease. I'm sure I don't have to tell you, but I will anyway," Mandalian said with a sideways glance, "that's what the Arapaho mix their warpaint with."

Matt tested the breeze, to no avail. "I can't smell anything."

"Neither can I right now, but it was there. I don't think we'd better waste a whole hell of a lot of time gettin' down that trail."

"What do you think's the best way to work it?" Matt asked. "Horses running and spaced about ten yards apart?"

"Yeah, about that. At least ten yards between mounts and ridin' hellbent for leather. As you go down, watch the bottom of the trail. There's a cut in the meadow there, where a little feeder stream comes in. It's deep enough to keep horses out of sight and still get to them in a flash if they're needed. That's the way the Arapaho like to work an ambush." Mandalian paused and brushed an imaginary speck of dust from the gold-beaded front sight of his rifle. "That is, if there are any Arapaho and if they got an ambush workin'."

"We'll assume your hunch is correct until proven otherwise," Kincaid said, twisting in the saddle to find his squad leader. "Okay, Corporal, let's get to it. You heard Windy. Space your troops at least ten yards apart. I'll be in the lead and—"

"Excuse me, Matt," Mandalian broke in. "Sorry to interrupt,

but I'd kinda like to head up this parade. I think it'd be best for all concerned if you brought up the rear, just in case somebody goes down or gets trapped somewhere between here and the bottom."

Matt studied the scout in silence for several moments. "All right, Windy, this is your show. You take the front, Corporal Wojensky the middle, and I'll bring up the rear." Matt glanced at Private Dobbs, whose six-foot-seven-inch frame appeared to have been draped in a gangling pile atop his horse. "And keep low, will you, Stretch?" he added softly. "You make one hell of a fine target."

The last words provided what Kincaid had hoped they would, bringing a low round of chuckles from the soldiers and breaking the tension that was rapidly building. He watched as the men checked their weapons, jockeyed their horses into assigned positions, then glanced over at Windy.

"Ready when you are, Windy. See you at the bottom."

Windy nodded and moved his horse to the edge of the meadow, where the rocky shale of the narrow trail led to the second meadow below them. With a final glance over his shoulder to make certain the eight horses behind him were properly spaced, the veteran scout suddenly slammed his heels against his horse's flanks, leaned low across its withers, and let out a blood-chilling scream that rattled off the walls of the cliff. The roan beneath him broke instantly into a gallop, plunging down the trail, sending rocks shooting up from its hooves.

The trooper immediately behind Mandalian, one Private Cavanaugh, who had served with the Confederate Army during the Civil War, let out a piercing rebel yell and his mount bolted down the trail, followed by the eight other horses. Mandalian was halfway to the bottom, with a hundred yards to go, when the first shot blasted up from the cut and slammed into the rocks behind his head with a crying whine. The scout snapped off a quick shot at the puff of smoke rising lazily into the air, jacked another shell into the Sharps, and fired again from beneath the horse's neck, staying low and keeping his mount between him and the as-yet-unseen enemy.

Several more blasts shattered the evening calm and more puffs of smoke rose from the meadow. Private Cavanaugh died with a second rebel yell rising in his throat, and pitched over the front of his mount, which catapulted head over heels with a bullet through its neck. Both horse and rider lay scattered across the narrow trail, and the next soldier reined in sharply to avoid colliding with his fallen comrade and spilling his horse over the dead animal lying at an angle to the trail and blocking passage.

The rest of the squad pulled their plunging, rearing mounts to a sliding stop and fired toward the cut while bullets from below splattered around them and ricocheted into the clear blue sky.

"Dismount and take shelter where you can find it!" Wojensky screamed as he jumped from his saddle and turned to face Kincaid and the other riders piling up behind him. "Trail's blocked, sir! Cavanaugh's dead, so is his horse, and they're lying across the damned trail!"

"Get into the washouts and return fire!" Matt yelled, squeezing off a round while seeing Windy's roan hit the meadow at the bottom of the trail at a dead run and angle away from the ravine with Windy firing over his shoulder as he moved away. Seconds later, two warriors were mounted on their ponies and streaking across the meadow behind the rapidly receding figure of the scout.

"Good," Matt muttered as he leaped down, "that's two of the bastards who won't be coming back." Kincaid turned his horse back up the trail and swatted it across the rump. "Turn your mounts loose to follow mine! They'll stop in the meadow above! There's no place to shelter them here!" Then he dove for an outcropping of rock as a column of dust and stones exploded where he had been standing.

The riderless horses clattered back up the trail, their heads twisting from side to side, their eyes rolling in their heads.

Private Ike Pappas fired once before lunging up from his prone position behind a small boulder and sprinting for a washout in the cliff wall some ten yards away. Immediately a bullet impacted against flesh, and Pappas' body spun in a whipping, twisting arc and he sprawled facedown on the trail while grasping his thigh and arching his back with cries of pain.

Kincaid crouched lower behind the outcropping and prepared to spring from the safety of his position. "Listen up, men! I'm going after Pappas. Lay down a regulated field of fire on that ravine. Wojensky? You and Dobbs and Minton fire first! The rest of you fire while they're reloading. Alternate like that until I get Pappas back here! Corporal Wojensky?"

"Yessir?"

"On the count of five, be ready to cover me!"
"Yessir!"
"One, two, three, four—" Kincaid's voice sounded hollow in his ears, and his body tensed while incoming rounds continued to slam into the rocks and sing their dying, screeching song. "Five!"
The three Springfields fired simultaneously and were quickly followed by a volley from the second three, while the first group reloaded before the echo of their shots had died. With the constant hail of lead pouring down, the cut was silent except for the occasional shot snapped off in haste with little chance for aiming. Kincaid sprinted forward and stooped over Pappas, the sweat dripping from his forehead and onto the wounded man's shirt as he rolled him onto his back to lift him beneath the armpits. One shot, lucky or aimed, tore through the left shoulder of Kincaid's tunic, ripping cloth and bringing an instant flood of crimson to the surface. Matt could feel the searing burn across his upper shoulder, but he ignored the pain and backed toward the outcropping, dragging Pappas behind him. The private was staring at the vacant sky, his white lips moving in a silent prayer.
"Hang on, Private," Matt grunted. "I'll either get you out of their sights or we'll be dead together."
Pappas rolled his head back to look up at the straining officer. "Thank you, sir. This is why . . . every soldier in Easy Company . . . considers you to be . . . to be the best officer in the whole . . . fucking army."
"Cut the bullshit and save your strength, Private," Matt snapped, embarrassed by Pappas' words. "There isn't any best officer. We're all just trying to do a job."
Pappas grinned through his pain. "I know, sir, and . . . and most of 'em ain't doin' worth . . . a . . . dandy hoot in hell at it, either."
The outcropping was beside them now, and Matt dragged Pappas behind the rocks, sheltered from direct fire, and quickly tore the soldier's trouser leg apart to examine the wound. Blood poured from the jagged hole, but there were no pumping gushes and Matt took instant relief from the fact that no arteries had been severed.
"How bad is it, sir?" Pappas asked softly.
"It's bad, but not as bad as it could be. I'm going to have to use a tourniquet to try and stop that bleeding."

"Will I lose my leg?"

Kincaid smiled cautiously as he stripped Pappas' belt from his waist. "Let's worry about your life first and your leg later, all right? Right now we've got to reduce that blood flow as much as possible. Lay quiet now, and rest."

Matt turned his head slightly toward the trail. "Corporal Wojensky?"

"Yessir?"

"Cease covering fire and resume selecting targets of opportunity! We want to keep them on their toes, but we just might be here awhile and we'd best conserve our ammunition."

"Yessir! Squad! Random fire! Pick your targets well and aim even better!"

Matt heard a grunted chorus of agreement and heard staccato firing replace the spaced volleys while his hands worked a stick through the belt and he began twisting the makeshift tourniquet. He glanced once toward Pappas' ashen face; the soldier had his eyes closed while his lips mouthed the silent prayer again. Matt turned back to his work and didn't look up until he heard the soldier speak again.

"Lieutenant Kincaid?" the hushed voice asked.

"Yes, Ike?" Matt said gently, using the uncustomary reference to a private's first name.

"Will we get out of this thing alive?"

"We intend to."

Pappas' eyes fluttered open. "My hitch is up in two days, did you know that?"

"I do."

"I don't want to quit, but the girl I'm engaged to, Sarah Williams, won't marry me if I stay in the service."

"That's too bad, Ike. Hate to lose you. Your promotion to lance corporal should come through any day now."

"I know, sir, and thank you for pushing it. But I've been offered a good job on the outside. Foreman on a cattle spread. Sara wants me to take it."

The blood had slowed to a mere dribble, and Kincaid locked the stick in place, then patted Pappas' other leg. "Do what you have to do, Ike."

"I love Sarah, and . . ." The soldier's eyes snapped open and cleared with instant alarm, and he shoved Kincaid to one side with a violent thrust. "Watch out, Lieutenant! Behind you!"

Off balance, Matt twisted to one side while his right hand snaked across his waist and came back with his Scoff cocked and rising to fire.

The young Arapaho fired in the same instant, and the shot intended for Kincaid's back slammed into the rock wall. Kincaid's .45 belched flame twice, and the Indian who had sneaked down the trail to take them from behind sailed backward off his feet, his hands clutching at two enormous holes in his stomach. A second warrior sprang up several yards away, and a bullet from Matt's revolver tore into his chest before he could raise the rifle in his hands to his shoulder. He spun in a staggering turn to the edge of the trail and fell, twisting and spinning, to the rocks below.

Matt waited with both revolvers drawn now, watching the trail to the rear in case more than two braves had slipped over the jagged stone divide at the front of the upper meadow. After five minutes he was sure the only two who had were dead, and he turned again to Pappas.

"You all right, Ike?"

"Yeah, I'm fine. That was close."

"Damned close. Thanks for saving my life."

Pappas smiled weakly. "Thank you for saving mine, sir."

"Lieutenant Kincaid!"

Matt recognized Wojensky's voice over the heavy pounding of riflefire. "Yes, Corporal! What is it?"

"Watson's been hit!"

"I'll be right there!"

There was a brief pause. "Ain't no use, sir. He's dead."

Kincaid leaned against the rocks and methodically began to reload his revolver while the muscles bunched along his jaw as he stared at the ground.

The deepening shadows of twilight crept around them, and there was silence from the cleft below. Not a shot had been fired for the last ten minutes, and Wojensky scrambled back to Kincaid's position on his hands and knees.

"Too bad about Watson," he said as he pressed his back against the rocks. "And Cavanaugh too. It's a shame to lose two good soldiers like that."

"Yeah, Corporal," Kincaid replied, running a hand wearily over his dusty chin. "It's a shame to lose anybody in this business, even if they're as worthless as tits on a boar hog."

Wojensky nodded and looked at Pappas. "How's the kid doin'?"

"He might make it."

"I hope so. What do you think Mr. Lo's up to, Lieutenant?"

"Don't know for sure. There's two dead ones back up the trail, and two went after Windy so that makes four. How many rifles did you make out firing from the ravine?"

"Five, maybe six."

"Make it six. We're seven left, not counting Windy, so we should have a little edge on them anyway. Either Windy's got something to do with their silence, or they've had enough. With all the lead we poured into the cut today, we might have gotten lucky and hit a couple more."

"That's a poor trade, sir," Wojensky said sadly. "Only six Indians, if we got a couple more, for two of my men."

"We weren't in exactly the best bargaining position, Corporal. Nobody hates to lose a man worse than I do, but if we can hold our losses to Watson and Cavanaugh before this thing is over, I'll consider us lucky."

"Where do you suppose Windy is? Dead, maybe?"

Kincaid peered around the outcrop and studied the ravine in an extended silence. "Maybe," he said finally, "but I doubt it. He's out there somewhere, biding his time and waiting for his chance. When it comes, we'd better be ready."

The lonely call of a nighthawk, perched near its nest and waiting for the closing darkness to bring out its prey, was the only sound to be heard, with the exception of the gurgling river. The moon, anxious for its chance to dominate the sky, had already risen above the horizon, and as Matt watched the full, round disk climb into the heavens, he knew their luck had not improved. He had wished for cloud cover and a chance to escape in the darkness.

"Look at that goddamned moon, sir," Wojensky said quietly. "Not a fucking cloud in the sky."

"Yeah. Under any other circumstances it would be a beautiful evening. As it is, I've never seen anything so ugly."

Wojensky grinned and said, "With the exception, maybe, of one of Windy's girlfriends."

Matt nodded and smiled. "Yes, that's a very distinct possibility." Then he sobered and looked toward the river again. "They'll infiltrate along the other side of the river tonight, if they're still there, and in the morning we'll be easy targets for them. Their guns are silent now, and I wonder if that's just a ploy to make us think they've quit the battle. What do you think, Corporal?"

"I think the rotten little bastards are still down there."

"I agree. Let's find out for sure."

Wojensky watched Kincaid closely. "How are you gonna do that, sir? Mr. Lo ain't no dummy. He won't go for any of that hat-on-a-stick shit."

"I know. And that's why I intend to provide him with a worthwhile target."

"What are you aimin' to do, Lieutenant?"

"I'm aimin', as you say, to give him a good enough target to arouse his interest while denying him a good enough target to score on. I'm going to dive and roll to that next outcrop down there. If I don't draw fire, I'll continue that until I get to the bottom. If I do draw fire, we'll know we're still pinned down." Kincaid paused and looked back with his hands gripping stone in preparation for his plunge into the nakedness of the trail. "If I draw exceptionally accurate fire, Corporal, you are in charge. Get these men back to the rest of the command the best way you know how."

"Yessir. But I think it would be better if I . . ."

Kincaid was gone before the sentence was completed.

He sailed through the air like a diver into water, and cushioned the impact on the rocky soil by landing on his shoulder and hip. A cloud of dust rose lazily as he rolled, turning three complete revolutions, and scrambled in a crouch to the shelter of the outcropping.

Silence. Not a shot was fired.

Kincaid wiped the sweat from his forehead and eyes with the swipe of a sleeve, spat a mouthful of grime and tiny gravel from his mouth, and unconsciously dusted off the front of his uniform while studying the terrain below. He judged the distance to the next shelter as at least twenty-five yards, and then, after making sure his revolvers were secure and tugging his hat down more tightly, he plunged into a second diving leap. As he dropped toward the ground, five booming shots rang out.

Dirt and rock flew and lead ricocheted off the cliff, but Matt hit the trail in a spinning roll, landed on his feet, staggered, then dove again as the Springfields behind him laid down an intense barrage of protective fire. Another volley, random this time, rang out from the cut as Matt sprang to his feet and sprinted for the sheltering rock.

He was panting now, drawing in tortured breaths, and he could feel the warmth and stickiness of blood running down his arm. With a quick glance he confirmed that he had not been hit again but had only reopened the wound he had received earlier. Then he forgot about the wound and cocked his head to listen to the dominating boom of a Sharps being fired from the opposite direction. A slow grin, both happy and relieved, spread across his smudged face. Snatching the Scoff and its companion from his holsters, he plunged onto the trail again.

Running in a stooped-over zigzag and firing with both .45s, Kincaid worked his way to the bottom of the trail and fired his one remaining bullet as he dove behind a large boulder on the edge of the meadow. The riflefire from somewhere beyond the cut continued with methodical precision while the Springfields from above continued slamming lead into the dark gash in the field of green.

While feverishly thumbing fresh rounds into his revolvers, Matt studied the ravine and could tell both by sound and muzzle flash that the return fire of the Arapaho had been split, with some weapons now having to protect the rear. Leveling his right arm along the boulder, he squeezed off three quick shots, but the Arapaho rifles had suddenly gone silent again.

Kincaid listened carefully. He could hear the thunder of hoofbeats on the prairie sod, and in the thickening gloom he could distinguish three ponies streaking away with riders pressed close to their necks. Matt waited several minutes before standing and moving cautiously toward the cut, holding his revolvers before him, cocked and ready. His heartbeat increased as he neared the lip of the ravine, and his ears strained to pick up any sound. Just as he stepped to the edge, he heard the rustle of clothing. Kincaid dropped to his belly and his fingers strained on the triggers of the revolvers in his hands.

"Hold it! You're under arrest by the United States Army!"

He could barely make out a broad, buckskin-covered back in the gloom, with its owner bent over some object at his feet. Then came the muffled grunt of a dead man being turned over and the last breath of air being forced from his lungs. It seemed as though the man in the cut-bank had not heard his order.

"Hold it right there, dammit! You're under arrest!"

The man straightened slowly, turned, and spat almost in disgust. "Hell, you don't need to arrest me, Matt. I'll go willingly."

"Windy? That you?"

"Rumor has it."

"You old son of a bitch," Matt growled, lowering the revolvers and climbing to his feet. "Why didn't you say something earlier?"

"Nothin' to say."

"Well, you damned near got your head blown off for lack of conversation."

"Can't think of a better reason to die," Windy said, turning again to the dead young warrior at his feet. Another lay a short distance away. "Think we ought to count coup on these boys? Might scare a lesson into the others."

"No. That would only encourage retaliation and revenge. Leave them like they are. The others will come back for them later." Kincaid eyed the scout suspiciously. "I was beginning to wonder if you'd gone over the hill on us."

Windy spat again. "I did. With two Indians right on my ass. Took a while to teach 'em a tracking lesson." The scout hesitated and there was something akin to regret in his voice when he continued, "They couldn't have been over nineteen years old, either of 'em. They won't be needin' no more lessons of any kind."

"It's the shits, isn't it? So senseless. We lost two men ourselves. Glad you came back when you did, or we might have lost more."

"Been out there quite a while. Wasn't no use to you, though, until you went into your drunk-chicken act up on the trail."

"What do you mean by that?"

"Couldn't get close enough to pin 'em down till you started floppin' around like a goose with its foot stuck in the ice. The guard they had posted to the rear couldn't help but turn and watch you make a fool of yourself. When he did, I moved in. Damned fine job, Matthew. That took a lot of courage."

"Courage and stupidity are often used interchangeably, my friend. That was pure stupidity."

"Yup. And a pig's ass ain't pork." Mandalian turned back to the dead brave at his feet. "Know who that is?" he asked.

"No, who is it?"

Windy stooped, lifted the man's leg, and pointed at his left foot. Kincaid studied the deformed, nearly clubbed foot encased in a specially constructed moccasin. His eyes went back to the scout after Windy placed the leg on the ground again.

"Lame Crow?" Kincaid asked.

"One and the same. Collins said he was Eagle Flies Alone's right-hand man. That means our friend had business to tend to elsewhere."

"Like the agency, maybe?"

"That's what I'm thinkin'."

"Goddamn," Matt said softly. "Davis has never been in a battle before. Hope he uses his head."

"If he don't, he figures to have a mighty bare spot on the top of it."

eight

Captain Conway watched her, a pretty young girl with brownish-blond hair and fragile, narrow hands that worked a linen handkerchief in nervous twists and tugs as she sat on a chair before the desk. Conway had just resumed his seat, having held the chair for the girl, and now he studied her thin, almost childlike body and wondered how she managed to exist in the rugged life they all shared. But when the girl looked up, there was determination and strength in her eyes.

"My name is Sarah Williams, Captain. I'm engaged to Ike Pappas."

"I'm pleased to meet you, Miss Williams. I'm Captain Conway."

"I know. Ike talks about you and Lieutenant Kincaid all the time."

Conway smiled. "I'm flattered, as I know the lieutenant would be. We think a lot of Private Pappas."

Sarah's eyes shifted and she glanced down for a second before looking directly at Conway again. "That's what I'm here to talk to you about, Captain. The part about his being a private."

Conway's brows wrinkled in confusion. "About what?" he asked.

"About Ike's being a private. I don't want him to be promoted, I want him to remain a private."

Conway was no less confused. He was used to married women complaining about the lack of promotion for their men, but this was the first time he ever had a fiancée complain about the possibility of her husband-to-be being promoted.

"I don't think we're communicating extremely well here, Miss Williams. I assume what you meant was that you think Private Pappas deserves a promotion."

"Oh, no. Not at all. I want him to stay a private."

Conway shook his head in dismay. "I don't think Pappas sees it that way, ma'am, and neither do I. He deserves a promotion to lance corporal, and if I can push it through channels, I'll see that he gets it."

The blue eyes across from him grew hard and Conway discarded any notion that she might be a frail little girl lost on the frontier. "What he deserves is a chance at life, Captain. You are depriving him of that chance."

"I am? In what way?" Conway asked, his patience with the entire conversation growing thin.

"By promoting him."

"By what?"

"You heard me, Captain. The promotion of Ike Pappas to lance corporal would be the greatest disservice you could do him."

Conway rubbed his knit brows. "I'm sorry, ma'am, I'm afraid I must have missed something along the way, so let me try to get this straight. You're engaged to Pappas, you want to be his wife, but you don't want him to get the promotion he deserves. You're happy with him as a private and you want him to stay that way. Is that correct?"

"No, it isn't. I'm not happy with him being a private."

Conway shrugged and slapped his open palms on the desk in helplessness. "Then what, if I may ask, would make you happy?"

Sarah Williams adjusted her skirts and looked away for a moment, and Conway thought he saw a hint of tears in her eyes. And in that moment he saw a vulnerability he had not seen before, and the hardness that had been dominant completely disappeared. Finally she turned to face him.

"I love Ike Pappas, Captain. I love him more than you could ever know, and Ike loves me."

Conway's impatience was replaced by nervousness and he cleared his throat self-consciously. "I'm—ahem—I'm delighted for you, Miss Williams. You and Private Pappas. But if you love him as much as you say you do, I can't understand why you're in opposition to his being promoted."

"You can't understand? It is *because* I love him that I don't want to see him get promoted."

Conway inhaled a deep breath and exhaled slowly as he leaned back in his chair. "I'm afraid we're going to have to start over, Miss Williams," he said wearily. "I don't profess to be the smartest man in the world, but—"

Just then he heard the door open and a familiar, feminine voice greeted Sergeant Cohen. Conway leaned forward with a start.

"Good afternoon, Sergeant Cohen," the pleasant voice said, and there was genuineness and sincerity in her tone. "I wonder if I might speak with the captain for a moment."

"Good afternoon, Mrs. Conway." There was the sound of the first sergeant's chair scraping back as he stood in her presence. "I'm sorry, but he has a visitor just now, and—"

"No bother, then. I'll come back later, when he isn't busy. It wasn't important and it can—"

"Please, please come in, Flora. I . . . I'd like for you to meet someone," said Captain Conway, having hurried to his office door. He was now moving forward to escort his wife into the office. Guiding her with his hand on her elbow, he leaned close to her ear and whispered through clenched teeth while maintaining a steady, straightforward stare, "Besides that, I can't understand a goddamned thing she's saying."

Sarah Williams looked up and saw approaching her the woman she had seen many times in the mercantile store and always admired from a distance. Flora Conway was stunningly beautiful, and even though she was in her mid-thirties, the years of traveling from post to post had served only to add dignity to her innate beauty, and her carriage was that of a dignified lady from the East, rather than that of a poor soldier's wife from a dismal outpost on the frontier.

"Miss Williams, I would like for you to meet my wife, Mrs. Conway. Flora, please meet Miss Sara Williams."

Flora extended her hand immediately and stepped forward with a warm, engaging smile on her face. "I'm very pleased to meet you, Miss Williams. May I call you Sarah? This 'Miss' and 'Mrs.' business seems so awfully stuffy. And please call me Flora."

Sarah Williams stood, grasped the extended fingers, offered a tiny curtsey, and then sat down quickly as though awed by the power of the lady to whom she had just been introduced. "Yes, I'd like for you to call me Sarah, ma'am," she mumbled.

"I've seen you in the store in town many times, Sarah," Flora said, choosing not to push the issue of her first name, "but we've never been properly introduced. I'm so glad you came by today. Once you've finished conducting your business with Warren, may I invite you to a cup of tea? Maggie, Sergeant Cohen's wife, and I were going to meet in fifteen minutes, as a matter of fact."

The relief on Conway's face yielded to urgency and he said quickly, "I think our business has pretty much been conducted, hasn't it, Miss Williams? For the time being at least?"

Sarah Williams looked at him and offered a tired smile. "Yes, Captain, I guess it has. As you said earlier, I don't think we communicated too well." She turned to look up at Flora. "Yes, ma'am, thank you. I would be delighted to have tea with you."

Flora smiled, took Sarah's arm, and led her toward the door while saying breezily over her shoulder, "Goodbye, Warner. For all your military brilliance, I think you have the young lady confused. Don't be late for supper."

When they were gone, Conway sank into his chair, reached for a cigar, and sighed heavily as he touched flame to tobacco. Sergeant Cohen appeared in the doorway and leaned against the jamb. "Got a minute, sir?"

With the cigar clenched between his front teeth, Conway looked up over the haze of smoke. "Sure, Sarge, come on in. Did you hear any of that?"

"I heard all of it, sir."

"Wasn't that something? How in Christ's name is a man supposed to understand what in hell she wanted?"

"Beats me, Captain. But I'm sure Mrs. Conway will get it straightened out."

Conway looked up with a sheepish grin. "You caught that too, eh?"

"That's what women are for, sir. To understand other women." Cohen hefted the sheaf of papers in his hand. "You haven't seen today's dispatches, have you, sir?"

"No. Hell no. I haven't had the time. What've you got?"

Cohen stepped forward and laid the top document on the captain's desk. "Orders from Regiment. Private Pappas is now Lance Corporal Pappas."

"Well," Conway said with a glance at the papers, "I'm damned happy for Pappas, but I don't envy him the chore of telling his little woman. Sounds like she'd be tickled pink to see him busted back to recruit. Regiment's timing couldn't have been much better."

Cohen turned toward the door. "As usual, sir. Late when

they should be early and early when they should be late."

"Anything on the payroll yet?"

"No, sir. Shall I send another message?"

"Of course. Send another and just keep sending them. They don't do any good, but it makes a man feel better if nothing else."

"That it does, sir."

Flora Conway was strangely silent throughout dinner and the remainder of the evening. Where she was usually jovial even in moments that would be distressful to most women, now her attitude was one of moroseness and melancholy. And when they prepared for bed, Flora seemed not to notice Conway's admiring glances, which he always gave, not as a payment, but through genuine awe and continued admiration for her beauty and figure, which should properly have been those of a lady at least ten years her junior. It was Conway's nature, perhaps a product of his Virginian upbringing or the commitment of an entire lifetime to the army, that made him wait for his wife to voice her complaints and any grievances that might be on her mind. He never asked if anything was wrong, because he knew that Flora was not only entirely capable, but entirely willing, to tell him if such were the case.

There was a virginal quality to the whiteness of her firm body as she stood there, naked before the mirror, and pulled a nightshirt over her head while Conway, in his longjohns, turned back the covers and slipped into bed. He watched Flora's dusultory effort to brush her long blond hair, which she held in a train over her right shoulder, and even in the strained silence he could feel the thrill of sexual desire pass through his loins as he watched his wife's reflection in the mirror.

"Warren?" Flora asked in a distant, thought-filled voice.

Conway continued to watch her for a moment. "Yes, love?"

"Could you keep a secret from one of your men?"

"I keep many secrets from them."

"I mean a particular secret from a particular man."

"That would depend on the man and the secret." Conway watched her more closely now, with narrowing eyes. "Would you care to tell me what and whom we are talking about?"

Lowering the brush to her side, Flora turned to face him. "We're talking about Ike Pappas and his promotion."

"Not that again."

"Yes, that again. Do you remember telling me about it at the dinner table tonight?"

"Of course I remember. It tickled the hell out of me, but it seemed to have a different effect on you."

"It did. And that's the secret I'm asking you to keep."

Curious now, Conway sat up and hooked his hands over his knees. "Would you mind being a little more specific?"

"I'm sorry, but this has me a little upset."

"I've noticed that."

Flora moved gracefully across the room to sit beside her husband on the bed and place a hand tenderly on his cheek. "Please don't be angry with me, and I'm sorry if I've caused you concern. Do you remember the girl who was in your office today? Sarah Williams?"

Conway nodded. "I don't think I could forget her. She talked to me for ten minutes and never said anything. What about her?"

"She's engaged to marry Ike Pappas."

"That much she was kind enough to reveal in her conversation. Good for her, Ike's a fine man, but she didn't seem too keen on seeing him get ahead."

"That's because she's afraid that if he gets promoted, he'll reenlist."

"So what?"

"Because she won't marry him if he stays in the army."

"She *what*?"

"That's right. If he reenlists, their engagement is off."

"That's love?" Conway asked with a mixture of disgust and curiosity.

"Very much so, for Sarah. Pappas has been overdue for promotion for—"

"We all have been, Flora. Pappas is no exception."

Flora smiled and kissed her man gently on the cheek. "I know, dear heart, I know, and you never complain, which I think is admirable. You should be a major, Matt should be a captain, Ben should be a legitimate first sergeant, I know all that."

"Pappas deserved that promotion and I'm damned glad to see him get it," Conway said, looking away.

"Even if it costs him his marriage?"

"That's his business and nobody else's."

"Then you're going to tell him about it?"

"Damned right I am. He's on patrol with Matt and the rest of First Platoon, but they should be back within the week. Pappas is due for discharge when he returns, and I'm sure Regiment pushed through this promotion as an enticement for him to stay. Whether he does or not is up to him. My job was to get the promotion for him and to inform him of that promotion at the first possible opportunity, which I intend to do."

Flora remained seated on the edge of the bed and continued to work the brush listlessly through her hair. "Do you know he's been offered a good job on the outside? Foreman of a big cattle ranch or something. He would earn twice what he makes now, even with the promotion."

"That's wonderful," Conway said derisively. "I don't think it's ever been considered a big secret that civilian jobs pay more than serving in the military."

"Do you think the promotion will be sufficient reason for him to stay in?"

"I don't know. It has been for others."

"Then he loses the woman he loves and the chance for a great future in civilian life. What a terrible position to be in."

Conway patted his wife's thigh tenderly and said, "As far as I'm concerned, Flora, if she loves him as much as she says she does, she wouldn't put him in that position in the first place. I've made my decision and you've stuck by me, through the bad as well as the good. If this Sarah were any kind of woman, she'd do the same thing for Pappas."

"But she doesn't like military life."

"Do you?" Conway asked. "Has this all been the height of your fondest dreams, or have you had to accommodate occasionally for the sake of our marriage?"

Flora smiled and a wistful look crossed her face. "You know the answer to that, dear heart. There is nothing I wouldn't do for you."

"Nor I for you. And that's why we've managed to endure the bad times and enjoy the good. Don't tell me that, as a ranch foreman, Pappas isn't going to run into some rough going. What is his precious wife going to do then? Leave him if everything isn't just right?"

"You're correct, dear heart, absolutely correct, as always," Flora said with a pleasant smile as she rose to lay the brush on the dresser. "When we had tea today she asked me to ask you to withhold any news of a promotion, if he got one, from

Pappas so he would quit the service. I knew it wouldn't be right even to ask that of you, but I was torn and greatly disturbed by that fragile little girl's love for her man. Maggie told me there was no sense in my even asking you, but I still felt I had to give it a try. Maggie was right and I was wrong and I apologize for having interfered."

Flora turned as she said the final words, and her breasts pressed against the soft material of the nightshirt. There was a glistening sheen to her blond hair in the lamplight, and she moved toward him with perfectly matched white teeth slightly parted behind full, rich lips. The thrill passed through Conway's body again, but this time it was intensified and nearly a shudder. She stopped just out of reach and toyed absently with the hemline of the nightshirt while her mouth formed the tiniest of pouts. "Can you forgive me?" she asked in a breathless whisper.

Conway ran the tip of his tongue over his dry lips and swallowed hard. There was a huskiness to his voice when he spoke, and the words came out as though his throat were too tight. "Yes," he managed, stepping from the bed and shrugging out of his longjohns, "but not with that damned shirt on."

"Warren," she teased, backing away, "now you be good."

"I intend to be," he replied, reaching out quickly and grabbing her wrist.

Flora feigned resistance as he pulled her toward him, but there was little enthusiasm in her struggle and her lips parted again while a deep longing filled her eyes.

Conway's lips were on hers and he kissed her with a hint of roughness while one hand went under the nightshirt, paused on her flat stomach, then moved upward to cup one breast tenderly. His thumb found her hardening nipple and turned in revolving orbits while pressing inward. Flora caught her breath as she broke off the kiss and her lips moved to his neck to search out his skin with nibbling kisses. She could feel the pressure of his groin as a large, hard object warm against her. "Warren, oh, Warren," she moaned, her lips moving to his ear.

Now Conway's hand moved downward again to caress the soft blond pubic hair momentarily before sliding between her thighs, which opened for him without reluctance. His fingers moved in wonderful, massaging, probing strokes and Flora's breathing came more quickly and she squirmed upon his hand.

With his free hand, Conway pulled her nightshirt off and dropped it to the floor while his tongue found her nipples and teased each of them in turn with darting flicks. Her knees were going weak and her arms went around his neck and she backed toward the bed and fell on it with eyes closed, her head thrown back and lips parted in ecstasy.

He moved inside her and they worked together, slowly for the first few minutes but with ever-increasing speed and desire until their bodies took control.

"Now!" Flora cried through tortured breath. "Now! Now! Now! Together, right now!"

Their bodies were molded as one, and their flooding, mutual climax caused a shudder to pass through them in that instant of blinding, passionate explosion. At that moment, Private Pappas' promotion could not have been further from Flora's mind.

Windy Mandalian cinched the last leather thong down and stood away from the travois to examine his work, comprised of blankets lashed to freshly cut poles. "Well, Pappas, it ain't no feather bed, but it just might get you back to civilization," he said, scratching his head and adding, "wherever in hell that is and whyever in hell you'd want to go there."

Pappas had been watching the scout work from where he lay on the grass, and he nodded with a weak smile. "Thanks, Windy. I've got a damned good reason to want to get back to civilization."

"So I hear. Congratulations."

"Thanks." Pappas looked away and his eyes misted from a pain that had nothing to do with his wound. "That is, if she'll want a cripple."

"You're only a cripple if you let yourself be, son," Windy offered with a grunt as he hoisted the saddle onto his horse's back. "Sure, you might not be able to run as fast as you used to, but you can still sit a horse with the best of 'em, and there ain't no reason for the army to treat you any different now than they have in the past. Same goes for a man's woman, if she's worth two bits in hell." He stooped to grab the cinch strap, then glanced over his shoulder and added with a grin, "I ain't seen many that were, but maybe you pulled a winner out of the barrel."

"*I* think I did."

"Then you did," Windy said, giving the cinch a final tug and lowering the stirrup from where it hung on the saddle horn. Then he turned to face Kincaid and a trooper who rode up leading the other mounts. "Looks like you got 'em all," he said to Matt.

Kincaid nodded, but his eyes were on the two cold figures wrapped in gray blankets and lying off to one side. "Yeah, we did. Damned shame there'll be two empty saddles when we get home."

"Can't change it, Matt. Gone is gone."

"Still a damned shame," Kincaid said, stepping down and turning to the soldier. "Corporal Wojensky's got the rest of the squad down guarding the trail to the meadow. Go get a man and come back here and load Watson and Cavanaugh across their saddles. We'll give them a decent burial back at the agency. Handle them carefully now, with the same respect you would give them if they were alive."

"Yessir," the soldier said, and there was an unmistakable quiver to his lower lip. "Watson was my best friend."

"Then you stay down there and send someone else back up."

"I . . . I can do it, sir. I—"

"Don't argue with me, soldier. All I need to hear from you is 'yes, sir.'"

The soldier snapped to attention. "Yessir."

"Get on with it, then," Matt said, and as the trooper moved away he called after him. "Boswell?"

"Yessir?" the trooper asked, stopping and turning.

"I'm damned sorry about your friend Watson."

"Thank you, sir. So am I."

They watched the young soldier disappear down the trail, and Windy said to Matt without looking at him, "Kinda hard on the troops this mornin', aren't you, Matt?"

"Yeah, I suppose so, Windy. But we lost two men on this patrol and Pappas is shot up. That's a third of the squad, and we're not even back to the agency yet. We've got to stay sharp if we're to survive, and the only way for a mounted infantry unit to stay sharp is to stay military."

"Guess so," Windy allowed. "Don't know much about that kinda thing myself."

"How are you feeling?" Matt asked, kneeling beside Pappas.

"Not tip-top, sir. Pretty weak, but I think I'll live."

Kincaid clapped the soldier gently on the shoulder. "Damned right you will. And you'll live to fight again another day."

"Thank you, sir," Pappas replied before looking away. "But it doesn't look like I'll be wearin' blue on blue when I do."

"That's entirely up to you, but whatever you're wearing, you're still going to have to fight. Like now. You're not out of the woods yet. Stay tough, stay mean, and you'll make it. Throw in a little weakness, a little self-pity, and you're a dead man." Kincaid straightened and there was a weariness on his face. "If this uprising is as bad as it looks, you just might see some more action before we get you home."

The two soldiers were lifting the dead onto their horses, and Pappas watched them for a moment before closing his eyes and biting his lower lip. "I hope not, sir. I'm hurtin' pretty bad and just a little sick of killing at this point."

"So am I, soldier. So am I. But it doesn't seem like we've got a hell of a lot of choice in the matter right now," Matt said, turning to Mandalian. "Give me a hand lifting Pappas onto your chariot there, Windy. Then we'd better move out. I'm not real pleased to think what we're going to find at the agency if the Arapaho have for a fact gone to war."

"What's war, Matt?"

"A lot of dead people."

"That's about it," Windy replied as he grasped Pappas carefully beneath the shoulders. "A lot of dead people."

nine

David Ramsey looked first at Lieutenant Davis and then at Doug Collins. He was covered with dust, and sweat trickling from his sideburns left glistening trails on his cheeks. He held a Winchester loosely in his left hand and nursed a mug of beer thirstily in his right. Then, brushing the foam from his mouth, he said without kindness, "Would either of you two fine officers of the United States Army mind telling me what the hell is going on around here? Those goddamned savages are burning up the countryside, shooting holes in your ridiculous agency here, jumping on my ass like flies on cowshit, and you tell me we can't go after them until your Lieutenant Kincaid gets back? Balls! They're on the warpath and I think it's high time we did the same."

Collins tugged on an earlobe and stared dismally at the broken window in his office. "I can't believe it. I just can't believe that these Arapaho, whom I've fed and taken care of, would turn on me like that," he intoned mournfully. "They're a beaten people. I just can't believe they would take up arms once again."

Ramsey smiled bitterly. "Believe it? What more evidence do you need, man? Will you believe it when you see some bastard Indian walking down the street with your scalp in his hand?"

"Now hold on a minute, Mr. Ramsey," Lieutenant Davis said, mustering all the authority he could manage in his tone. "We don't know for certain how widespread this uprising is. We will catch the men responsible for this in time, but until—"

"In time! Is that going to put the grass back on the prairie, make your dead soldiers get up and walk around again, or put Merle, one of my best hands, back in the saddle instead of rotting back there where we left him, with a bullet through his forehead? Hell no, it isn't."

"I can't understand what the burning is all about," Collins

threw in, still confused and more than a little hurt. "Maybe it's a diversion for other raids, I don't know. Maybe I should wire Washington and tell them we've got a full-scale uprising on our hands. But—"

"'But' your ass, and fuck Washington!" Ramsey snarled as he slammed his mug down on the counter. "All we would get out of them is more pussyfoot and bullshit." He turned suddenly toward Davis. "And where the hell is this marvelous Lieutenant Kincaid? While we sit here on our butts and wait for him, the scum that killed my hand are riding away like church just let out."

"The lieutenant has gone to find the old man who is supposed to have started this whole mess. He's a medicine man named Gray Bear, and according to Mr. Collins here, he's ridden into the hills to seek a vision of some sort."

"A vision? Of what? My sister flat on her back, with her legs tied apart and fifteen Arapaho lined up to mount her? I say we take them now before they have a chance to do the same things they've done in the past and what the savage bastards will always do until they are no longer left to roam free like a pack of coyotes."

Lieutenant Davis stiffened himself to his maximum height of five feet ten and looked up at the tall young rancher. "For the time being, I represent military law in this district, and any actions you take contrary to my wishes will be considered an act of treason. I am under orders to defend this agency and the federal property located here, and until I deem that order has been restored, I am conscripting you and your men to aid me in that purpose."

Ramsey watched the young lieutenant while a scoffing snort escaped his lips. "You're *what?*" he asked in disbelief.

"You heard me, sir. You and your men will follow my orders."

"Hear that, boys?" Ramsey asked with a contemptuous chuckle in the direction of his men drinking beer toward the rear of the agency. "We're in the goddamned army."

"Like hell!" said a rangy, well-muscled rider with hair touching the nape of his neck and a scar running along the side of his cheek. "Never had much of a stomach for bluebellies in the first place, and I'm damned if I'm gonna *be* one."

Davis' face reddened and he spoke with lips tightening in resolve. "You, sir, wouldn't make a pimple on a mounted infantryman's ass! Furthermore, I don't care what you *want*. I'm only interested in what you will *do*, and that is to follow my orders."

The troopers who had been lounging outside the door began to file into the agency. They lined up behind their lieutenant with silent, ominous glances toward the cowboys, who placed their beer mugs aside and stood in preparation for whatever might come.

"Lieutenant," Sergeant Olsen said softly, "if you'll just give us a few minutes alone with these glorified sodbusters, we'll break 'em into the army right and proper."

The cowboys and soldiers were edging closer now, and Ramsey grinned in expectation.

"There will be none of that, Sergeant," Davis said over his shoulder, while continuing to watch the rancher. "And you, Mr. Ramsey, will be expected to keep your men under control, just as I will my troops. Is that understood?"

They watched each other silently, eyes locked for long moments, before Ramsey smiled and waved a hand toward his men. "Back off, Lars. It's true these soldier boys need to be brought down to size, but we'll play along with the lieutenant's wishes for a little while. But only for a little while," he said, turning to Doug Collins. "Set up a round of beer for everybody, including the army there. That is, if the lieutenant will allow his boys a little drink."

Collins looked first at Ramsey and then at Lieutenant Davis. "How about it, Lieutenant?" he asked, moving toward the beer keg.

"Certainly. My men deserve a drink, as do the others. But I will buy it with my own personal funds."

"You're all right for an army stiff," the man called Lars said as he and the other cowboys swaggered to the counter with empty mugs in hand. "Nothin' I'd like better than to get drunk on government money."

The fight didn't start until two hours later. Lieutenant Davis had gone to check the guard mount posted on the various buildings, and he would later remember that he had been gone no more than fifteen minutes. Although he had seen Sergeant Olsen and the cowboy named Lars exchanging surly glances, he thought everything was under control and that the men deserved a little break from the tension of the moment. And by the time he heard the first crash of breaking glass, it was already too late. Later, he was able to piece together the details of the brawl:

The soldiers were crowded at one end of the counter with the range hands jostling for position at the other end. In the center, between the two groups, stood Olsen and Lars, shoulder to shoulder. Even though no challenging words were spoken, they matched each other, drink for drink. There was an eerie silence about the room at first, in an atmosphere charged with tension and anticipation. When one of the soldiers referred to Sergeant Olsen by name, the big cowboy named Lars looked him up and down quizzically. It was obvious that both men were nearly equally matched in size and weight, with thick corded muscles in their arms, and broad, heavy shoulders straining the shirts across their backs.

"Olsen?" Lars asked with contempt. "You don't look like no Swede to me."

"That's because I'm not, thank God, and I'll thank you to keep your ignorance to yourself. I'm Norwegian, boy, a product of Trondheim, the land of the Vikings."

"'Boy'? Did I hear you say 'boy'?"

"I didn't say Roy."

The silence in the room became nearly a vacuum now, as though a single word spoken, or alien sound made, would suddenly cause the room to implode. Lars drank his beer in silence, as did Olsen, and both men stared straight ahead.

Finally Lars asked, "Norwegian, did you say?"

"That's what I said, and I'm surprised a man of your towering stupidity could pronounce the word."

"You know what a Norwegian is, boys?" Lars asked his cohorts without looking at them.

"No, Lars. What is it?" one them replied with a chuckle.

"It's a Swede with his brains knocked out."

The cowboys laughed heartily and the soldiers waited in silence.

Olsen raised his glass and held it before him as if he might be offering a toast and said in a rolling singsong, "Ten thousand Swedes ran through the weeds, chased by one Norwegian. He caught their ass there in the grass and whipped 'em fair and clean. Ten thousand more rose up and swore, 'That's the best damned fight I've seen!'"

It was the soldiers' turn to roar, and the cowboys respectfully held their silence and waited for their man's retort.

But Olsen wasn't waiting, and he asked, after the laughter died, "Hey, lads? You know what we do in Norway when a kid is born with his asshole right smack between his eyes?"

He was answered by elaborate shrugging and head-scratching.

"We ship him off to Sweden. That's how they get their kings."

The soldiers roared with laughter again, and the cowboys became impatient with the unbalanced repartee. "Come on, Lars," one implored. "Nail the bastard down."

But Lars's store of cute comebacks had dried up on him, and he stood there quietly with the red creeping up his neck, like mercury in an overheated thermometer. And when he finally did speak, the words escaped his lips in a controlled growl. "There ain't a Norwegian born what could match a Swede, punch for punch."

"Proof's in the pudding, cowboy, and I'll give you first punch, seeing as how you look like the pudding," said Olsen, turning toward the Swede. "Go ahead, boy, fire your best shot."

"I don't want no favors from you," Lars snarled, jutting his chin out as he turned. "Have at 'er, son. I'll take the second go 'round."

Olsen shrugged his shoulders and said, "Like I told you, I'm overwhelmed by your ignorance." And with that he teed off with a vicious right-hand punch that landed squarely on the big Swede's jaw and rocked him back on his heels. Lars worked his mouth, testing to see if his jaw was broken, which it wasn't.

"Not bad, for second-rate," he said, rocking forward on the balls of his feet and bringing his right fist around in a vicious, looping punch. His knuckles smacked against Olsen's jaw and the impact sounded like an oak limb being slammed against the stump of a tree. The sergeant took half a step backward and adjusted the hat that had tilted over his right eye. He spat a tiny trickle of blood from the corner of his mouth and said with disgust, "I got kids at home that can hit harder than that."

Lars glowered and raised both fists chest-high. "You have, have you now? Well, let's see what you can do with two hands, if you got the stomach for it."

Olsen was ready without an instant's hesitation, raising his fists and hooking a left to the Swede's rock-hard belly with crushing power. Lars countered with a crossing right that glanced off Olsen's forehead. The two men stood toe-to-toe, throwing vicious lefts and rights, neither of them backing up an inch. In a scene much like two mountain rams slamming their horned heads together in ritual combat for supremacy of the herd, so too did Olsen and Lars go at each other hammer and tongs. Ugly red welts rose beneath their eyes and turned a dark blue-black, lips cracked and blood flowed, and knuckles turned red, skinned raw and bleeding.

Ramsey watched the fight with pleasure obvious on his face, and after nearly five minutes he turned to his riders, who were cheering their man on while edging closer to the fray. "What are you boys waiting for? Swede's got his half of the army, get the hell on in there and get your half."

The soldiers were quick to oblige, and the two sides leaped across the narrow opening between them with fists flying, knees slamming into groins and heads smacking against each other. And when Collins finally came to his senses and fired two rounds from a shotgun into the ceiling, chairs and tables lay strewn around the room like kindling, the stove was turned on its side with its stovepipe dangling precariously from the roof, and the floor was slick with blood and covered with bodies of men continuing to punch, bite, and kick from where they lay. In the center of the room Olsen and Lars stood, gulping in raw breaths of air and staring at each other, both with arms too tired to swing another blow.

Sergeant Olsen mopped the sweat and blood from his eyes with the back of a sleeve, then offered his hand to Lars. "Not a bad scrap, considering the conditions," he said.

Lars grinned through broken lips and touched his mouth gingerly with the back of his hand before reaching out and accepting the handshake. "Not bad at all. Makes a man mighty thirsty, though. What say I buy you a beer, soldier?"

Olsen grinned back and draped an arm over Lars's shoulder. "Guess I mighta been wrong, callin' you stupid the way I did. That's the smartest damned idea I've heard all day."

Collins raised his hands and backed away in protest. "Not on your life! You people are worse than Indians when you get your belly full."

Ramsey's face went blank and he leveled the Winchester in his hands. "Give the boys a drink, mister. All of 'em. Send your bill for the booze and the damages to the Bucking R ranch. I'd be more than proud to pay it."

And that was when Lieutenant Davis stumbled into the room. He nearly fell on the blood-slick floor, but he skidded to a stop and looked around the agency in amazement. The only article of furniture left in one piece was the long counter in the center of the room, where cowboys and soldiers stood side by side, bruised, bleeding, and broken, but drinking together with arms around one another's shoulders, laughing and talking as if they had been lifelong friends.

"What the hell's going on here?" Davis demanded, risking another cautious step or two in Ramsey's direction.

"Nothin', Lieutenant. The boys are just having a beer," Ramsey said with a pleasant smile.

"Nothing, my ass! We're supposed to be fighting Indians, not each other, dammit!"

Sergeant Olsen turned with a crooked grin. "Weren't any Indians available, sir."

Davis turned to Ramsey. "I demand an explanation, Mr. Ramsey. I specifically told you—"

"Fuck off, Lieutenant. This isn't West Point and I'm not playing soldier. You want to fight some Indians in the morning, I'm all for it, and this is just the crew that can do it for you. They'll fight better, now that they've got some respect for one another. Now belly on up here and have a beer and shut up with your military bullshit, or you and I are gonna go a round or two ourselves."

Davis stared at Ramsey's cold, expressionless eyes for nearly a minute before turning to Olsen. "Sergeant. We will be changing guard mount in exactly one-half-hour. I suggest you have a detail prepared and capable for duty."

"You've got it, sir. Now why not step up here and have a beer with us?"

Davis looked around the room again with an expression of hopeless despair. He started to speak once, then thought better of it. Finally he shrugged his narrow shoulders and moved up between Lars and Olsen. "What the hell's the use?" he said, trying to smile. "Out here the only thing the rule book seems to be good for is butt-wipe."

Olsen moved to one side to give the officer some room in the crush of bodies. "That it would, sir. And it sometimes does."

ten

Exposed as he was on the open prairie, the sun beat down on his bare, brown back and there was a glistening sheen of sweat across his wide shoulders. A tiny pinch of dirt cascaded over the side of the deepening pit, and Private Malone looked at the spoon in his hand with disgust bordering on hatred. "Would you believe a goddamned spoon to dig a mother-lovin' six-by-six with, now, I'd be askin' ya," he said to himself. "If the devil's mother'd had two bleedin' babies, one of 'em for sure would be Sergeant Coh—"

"Is that hole six foot on a side, Private?" asked a deep voice from above the pit.

Malone looked up with a start. "Why, good mornin' to ya, Sergeant Cohen. It is for a fact, sir—"

"Don't 'sir' me, soldier! I'm no goddamned officer! It's 'sergeant' to you."

"Beggin' your pardon, *Sergeant*. Beggin' your pardon indeed. Must be the sun's addled me brain."

"The question of whether you have a brain or not has been the subject of much speculation, Malone. I asked you, is that pit six-by-six-by-six?"

"It is for a fact, Sarge. At least the first two sides. I'm still workin' on the last one, don't ya know."

"I can see that. Is there any chance that this little exercise might dampen your enthusiasm for fightin' every swingin' dick in town when you get a little booze in your belly?"

Malone grinned and there was almost boyish innocence on his rugged face. "That'd be a piece of history, Sarge, sure enough. It don't take a Malone from County Cork long to learn the evil of his ways. You'd be lookin' at a reformed man, Sarge, I swear it on me sweet mother's grave."

"Yeah, and I have a fair idea of who put her there," Cohen replied with a snort. "I wouldn't stack that dirt too far from the hole, Malone, and I mention this only because you haven't made too great a display of intelligence since I've known you.

Remember, you're going to have to put it back in the hole again the minute you're through."

"And I'd be thankin' ya for the kindness of the reminder, Sarge. A fact it'd be that sometimes the little things get overlooked in the heavy goin'."

"Yeah. Like following orders. Captain Conway said he might come out later on to see how you're getting along, so look sharp when he does."

Malone snapped to attention where he stood in the pit, and held the spoon across his chest at present arms. "Me weapon is clean and ready for inspection, Sarge."

Cohen shook his head in disgust. "Carry on, Malone. With you, it's impossible to tell humor from ignorance."

The sergeant turned and walked back toward the post, some fifty yards away, and Malone watched him momentarily before stooping again to his task. "'Tis a waste of an honest man's labor, that's what it'd be," he groaned, jabbing the spoon into the dark prairie soil and tossing another tiny deposit over the side of the hole. "Not to mention being damned thirsty work. I'd give a month's pay and kiss the cook's ass at high noon and give him an hour to draw a crowd just for a pint—no, make that two—of ale."

As the afternoon wore on, Malone's pit inched deeper toward the required six-foot level and he straightened to lean against the wall for a moment's rest. Screwing the top off his canteen, he took a long drink of the tepid water and arched his back to relieve the throbbing ache in his lower spine. He had worn out one spoon and was working on his second, which he stared at mournfully between draughts from the canteen. Malone heaved a weary sigh, screwed the cap back on, and leaned down to begin again when he heard feminine voices coming from a distance, carried on an afternoon breeze.

Turning toward the sound, he saw Maggie Cohen—a woman whom he deemed to be equally as tough as her husband, the first sergeant—and the sutler's squaw walking back toward the outpost from the tipi ring that constituted the Indian encampment some three hundred yards from the post's northeast corner. Only because Pop Evans, the sutler, was the trader on post who sold beer, and because he had the best-looking squaw to be found in the area, Malone leaned his elbows on the pit wall and envied the man for a moment. The two women, chatting happily and thoroughly engrossed in their conversation, moved toward him without obvious care or concern.

They were but fifty yards from Malone's pit when he heard the rumble of hooves on the prairie and his head jerked toward the sound. A huge longhorn bull trotted to a stop, pawed the earth several times, and rolled its head as it sniffed the breeze. Malone watched the bull and could see the sun glinting off the tips of its wide horns. White foam dripped from the corners of its mouth. And he knew instantly that the bull had gone crazy and was preparing to attack the two women, who, oblivious to danger, continued to walk casually toward the outpost.

Grabbing his tunic, Malone leaped from the pit and sprinted toward the ladies.

Maggie Cohen's eyes darted in puzzlement toward the massive, half-naked man running toward them. The bull was charging now, closing the distance from the rear, its horns held low, and she heard the animal for the first time. Both women turned, and a startled scream shattered the stillness as Malone ran past them to position himself between the ladies and the bull. He held his tunic in front of him like a cape, while yelling over his shoulder, "Don't run, Mrs. Cohen! Let me draw the bull away first, then hightail it to the post!"

"Please be careful, Mr. Malone!" Maggie called, watching the bull break stride and veer toward Malone.

Malone didn't reply as the bull charged toward him and hooked a horn into the space where the Irishman had been a moment before, but had vacated at the last second with a sideways leap. Its horn pierced the tunic as the bull reared its head, and the shirt was torn free from Malone's grasp. The bull hesitated momentarily, with the blue material hanging down by one ear, and shook its head to clear its vision. It stood between the ladies and Malone now; undecided, it looked back and forth with blood-red eyes, drool hanging from its mouth in stringy threads.

Malone clapped his hands and feigned a charge toward the enraged animal while shouting, "You'd be lookin' for a fight would ya, ya ugly brute! Come and get it! Meet me halfway, ya splotch-faced coward!"

As though the bull had understood the verbal challenge, it wheeled toward Malone and charged again, missing Malone's midriff by nothing more than inches as he danced away again. But the bull's back was to the ladies now, and Malone risked a glance in their direction.

"Run like ya never run before, Mrs. Cohen," Malone yelled while the clapping of his hands continued to hold the bull's attention. "He'll be turnin' your way with the next bloody pass!"

Maggie Cohen and her companion raced toward the safety of the outpost with skirts held high and bloomers flashing on pumping legs, while the bull, getting madder with each passing second, charged again. Malone waited until the last moment before dancing to one side again, but the toe of his boot caught on a clump of sod and he lost his balance for a split second. Dagger-tipped, yellow horn pierced his pants leg and tore a shallow trench across the outer side of his upper thigh. There was an instantaneous flash of pain, and blood immediately turned the blue material to a dark crimson. Sensing that it had wounded its foe, the bull turned short, hooked its horns high, then lowered its head and charged again.

Ignoring the pain, Malone regained his balance and, crouching in a boxer's stance, faced the bull head-on. His right fist came back with the bull not five feet away, and he waited for that precise moment of hesitation before the longhorn raised its head to strike. And when it came, Malone slammed a devastating punch against the bridge of the bull's nose, just between the eyes, and jumped to one side again. The bull staggered and the momentum of its charge brought the animal to its knees in a skidding slide on the slick grass. Malone turned and, just as the animal was struggling to regain its footing, leaped onto the bull's neck. Grasping a horn in either hand, he braced his feet and twisted with all his might.

It was a battle of brute strength against brute strength, with the thick, heavy muscles of the bull's neck pitted against Malone's bulging, straining arms. Malone gritted his teeth. The sweat poured into his eyes from his brow, and he mustered up a reserve of power for one final, lunging twist. Then came a sharp cracking sound, and the head in Malone's hands twisted freely to the sky.

He stepped to one side and the bull went down with its left horn buried in the sod. The longhorn's tail twitched several times and its legs flailed helplessly before a mighty shudder passed through its frame and it lay still on the prairie. Malone was gulping huge breaths of air as he leaned forward to rest his hands on his knees and await the return of his strength. He didn't know the walls were lined with soldiers watching his solitary battle, nor did he see Sergeant Cohen racing toward him with a rifle in his hands. All he could think of was a cold glass of beer.

Cohen's steps slowed as he neared the exhausted Irishman, and he lowered the Springfield. He couldn't control the look of amazement in his eyes as he looked first at the dead bull and then at Malone.

"Private Malone," he said softly but with a hint of authority, "how many times do I have to tell you, you've got to knock off this goddamned fighting?"

Malone's head jerked up, and his eyes were red from sweat. "Now look, Sarge, I won't be takin' a whole lot of—"

"I'm just shittin' you, Malone. That was a hell of a fine thing you did, and I thank you. But tell me one thing. Your guns were lying right beside the pit, I saw them this morning. Why didn't you use one of them instead of your fists?"

There was a blank look on Malone's face as he replied, "Don't know. Guess I didn't think about it. Didn't have a hell of a lot of time. Mrs. Cohen and old Pop's squaw was in a peck of trouble when I seen 'em."

"Every man to his own poison, I guess," Cohen said, shaking his head. "That's the *first* thing I would've thought of."

Malone sucked in another deep breath and stood to full height and leaned back with his hands on his hips, as yet having totally ignored the wound on his thigh. "Well, we got 'er done anyway, Sarge. Guess it don't matter how ya kill 'em, just as long as they're dead."

It was then that Cohen noticed the blood-soaked right leg, and he stepped forward saying, "Looks like you got a little too close to your work there, Malone. I'd better have a look at that leg."

Malone glanced down, then tested his leg with a step. "Nothin' to it, Sarge. A pissed-off mosquito could've done better, I'm thinkin'."

"Just the same, let me have a look at it," Cohen said, laying his rifle on the grass and kneeling beside Malone to tear the pants leg away. He studied the wound for a few seconds, then stood again. "It's an open wound with a good flow of blood, so you should be all right. But we'd better get it cleaned up a bit and wrapped in some clean bandages. I'm sure Mrs. Cohen would be pleased to take care of that for you."

"If you'll pardon me, Sarge," Malone said, looking down

in embarrassment, "it don't seem proper to have a man's wife fussin' over another man's leg. The cook's doctorin' will suit me just fine."

Cohen shrugged. "Like I said, every man to his own poison." The first sergeant looked at what was left of Malone's tunic, still hooked on the dead bull's horn, and then at his torn trousers. "Doesn't seem to be much left of your uniform, Private. I suppose I'll have to overlook destruction of government property this time and issue you a new one."

Malone grinned. "If you'd be wantin' me to wear one, Sarge, I'm thinkin' that's bloody well what you're gonna have to do."

As they walked back to the outpost, Malone refused the sergeant's help and stopped by the pit to collect his weapons and his canteen. Then, as he hobbled through the main gate, the men on the wall sent up a wild cheer and nearly the entire post turned out to welcome Malone's safe return. Because of his reputation as a fighter, his devastating strength and simmering Irish temper, Malone was not always the most popular of men with the other soldiers, and now he grinned sheepishly, embarrassed by all the adulation.

Pop Evans rushed out of his store and pressed a mug of beer into Malone's hand while clapping him on the back and thanking him profusely for having saved the squaw. Malone nodded and downed the beer in a single gulp, and as he wiped the foam away from his mouth with the back of a hand, Maggie Cohen bustled across the parade with clean bandages folded across her arm and a pan of hot water in her hands.

Malone handed the mug back to Pop Evans and backed away with a terrified look in his eyes. "I'll be thankin' ya, ma'am, but me leg's just fine. I'll have old Dutch take a look at it when he gets his head out of the bean pot, but I'm thankin' ya for the trouble."

Maggie Cohen watched him with an ominous glint building in her green eyes. "You'll be doin' no such thing, Mr. Malone, and I'll be pleased to match me Irish temper to yours anytime. You saved me life today and I'll not be havin' you cared for by some incompetent. This pot's hot and gettin' a wee bit heavy. Now, away to my quarters with you, and off with those filthy trousers."

Malone looked helplessly at Sergeant Cohen, but Cohen only grinned with a helpless shrug. "I've lived with the lady a lot of years, Private, and the first thing I learned was not to argue with her. While I know you can whip a wild longhorn, I think the smart money in this case would have to be on Mrs. Cohen."

"Enough of this jibber-jabber, Benjamin," Maggie said with an impatient jerk of her head toward the noncom's quarters. "The man's been injured, any fool can see that. The quicker he's tended to, the better. Mr. Malone, follow me, if you please."

Private Malone very much resembled a lamb being led to slaughter as he followed Maggie to the top sergeant's quarters while the remainder of the company watched him in grinning approval.

When Malone stepped back onto the parade a half-hour later, the right leg of his trousers and longjohns had been cut away and a sparkling white bandage encircled his thigh. His blood-filled boot had been removed as well, and he walked in a gingerly hobble, not from the pain of his wound but because the tender bottom of his bare foot seemed to find every sharp stone in his path.

Maggie Cohen tossed the reddish water away with a swirl of her pan, and followed Malone nearly to the center of the parade.

"How does it feel now, Mr. Malone?" she asked with motherly concern.

"Fine, ma'am. Just fine. I'd be thankin' ya for the doctor work."

"Oh, posh. That was nothing. I'm just thankin' the Lord that horn wasn't just a wee bit farther to the right."

Malone wanted desperately to get away from this overpowering woman, and he crumpled his hat in his hands while offering a tiny dip of his head. "Thank you, ma'am. Nothin' to it and I'm sure it'll be just fine."

"Now you come back in two days and let me change that dressing, you hear?"

"Yes, ma'am," Malone mumbled. He saw the top sergeant angling toward them; it was the first time in his life he had ever been glad to see the man.

"How's the patient?" Cohen asked his wife.

"Fine, but stubborn as a mule. Just like all the rest of you men."

"But with the heart of a kitten, to be sure, ma'am," Malone said with a grin.

"Bet me on that," Maggie said with a toss of her head. Then

she saw the shovel in her husband's hand and arched her eyebrows quizzically. "What's that for, Ben?"

Cohen handed the shovel to Malone. "For the good private here. I've changed my mind, Malone. You can retire your spoons and finish your six-by-six with this."

"You'd be a sweetheart of a man, Sarge," Malone said, hefting the shovel. "All bloody wool and a bleedin' yard wide."

"Benjamin!"

"You run along and do your chores, love," Cohen responded to Maggie's angry exclamation. "You handle the mother work and I'll take care of the soldiering."

Maggie spun on her heel and stalked away with an angry shake of her skirts.

Cohen watched the hefty woman's bustling retreat and Malone said, "She's a beauty, Sarge, but I'm glad you're runnin' this outfit and not her, if you'll pardon my sayin' so."

"So am I, Malone. So am I. Take the rest of the day off. You can finish your detail in the morning."

Using the shovel as a crutch, Malone hobbled away. "Like I said, Sarge, you're a mile of heart."

Later that night, over the supper table, the top kick of Easy Company was ignored as though he were less than an unwelcome guest. Cohen chewed a mouthful of stew thoughtfully and washed it down with a gulp of coffee before looking across at his wife.

"I take it I'm not your most favorite person this evening."

"You're not," Maggie replied coldly as she toyed with the food on her plate.

"I suppose the next most intelligent question to ask would be 'why?'"

Maggie's eyes flashed when she looked up. "You know why as well as I do, Benjamin Cohen. You've become a hard man. Your heart has turned to stone."

"Because of Malone?"

"Because of Mr. Malone."

"Because he saved your life?"

"Because he saved my life and the fact that he's a lonely man who happens to have a wounded leg and shouldn't be made to dig any more stupid holes that have no purpose beyond punishment."

Cohen carefully wiped his mouth, laid his napkin aside, and

pushed his plate away. "Excellent dinner."

"Thank you."

"You're welcome," Cohen said, reaching into his pocket and pulling out a brown cigar. After he struck a match and took his first drag, he shook the flame out and looked at his wife again. "Malone, and men like him, are a strange breed of cat, Maggie. They're tough men who have no other life than the army, but they're children in a way. The only two things they understand are discipline and reward. They respect only strength, and in no way will they respond to weakness except in the negative sense. Malone knows how much I appreciate what he did. My giving him that shovel in exchange for his spoon told him that, but it also told him that company punishment is company punishment and must be carried out. When the first sergeant gives an order on an outpost like this one, he'd better damned well see that it is obeyed to the letter or his respect is gone. Without that, he is nothing."

"Even for wounded men who wouldn't be wounded if they hadn't saved that first sergeant's wife from certain death?"

Cohen nodded. "Even then. If things were different, I'd give Malone a two-week furlough and a hundred dollars out of my own pocket for what he did. But things aren't different. This is still the army, we're still assigned to Outpost Number Nine, and the daily struggle for survival goes on. Survival on an army post begins and ends with discipline." Cohen reached for the ashtray and tapped an ash from his cigar, then looked up with a grin. "But that doesn't mean we can't overlook a few things."

Maggie glanced up from the desultory stirring of her food. "What would you be meanin' by that?"

Cohen winked at his wife and there was a devilish glint in his eyes. "I'm not the only one who's indebted to Malone for what he did. Old Pop Evans is more than a little pleased to have his bed-warmer safe and sound. What with pay coming in late as usual, the troops have had to buy everything from his store on credit and he has to charge interest, as allowed by his contract with the government, if for no other reason than to save face with the men. Like I said, they don't respect weakness.

"But tonight he is going to serve beer for one hour at no cost in honor of Private Malone. Also, his squaw just happens to have a friend who's coming to the post tonight to see the private, and the quartermaster has arranged for Malone to use a spare bunk in the bachelor officers' quarters." Cohen winked again. "You know, so Malone can nurse his wounds in private? Pop Evans has also arranged for a bottle of whiskey to be waiting in that room. Of course I had nothing to do with any of this, and the fact that the officer of the day has chosen to ignore the fact that Malone will miss bedcheck is entirely coincidental."

It started with a giggle deep in Maggie's throat, and then rose to a hearty laugh as she threw her head back and roared with delight. Cohen smoked in silence, but there was a happy grin on his face. When Maggie finally gained control again, there were tears in her eyes and she swept around the table to kiss Cohen hugely on the lips.

"You'd be a cunning man, Mr. Cohen, yes you would. And I love you for it."

"You do? How much?"

"Just let me clear the dishes away and I'd be more than happy to show you."

"And I'd be more than happy to be shown."

Maggie kissed him again with increasing passion before turning to her work. "Just be patient, my magnificent soldier, and you shall have proof beyond your wildest expectations."

Cohen grinned, took a drag from his cigar, and watched the drifting smoke. "From hero to goat, from goat to hero," he said wistfully. "That's the story of a first sergeant's life."

Maggie stopped and turned with a dish in either hand. "I'd much rather make love to a hero than a goat, my dear. You just continue your heroics and leave the bleating to others less qualified."

Sergeant Cohen stubbed out his cigar and moved toward the bedroom while slowly unbuttoning his tunic. "I wish it were that easy, my love," he said. "I wish it were that easy. I haven't been able to get our pay out of Regiment, and tomorrow Captain Conway is going over there to find out why Easy Company can't get paid on time like any other army unit. It's a battle that seems to be never-ending."

Captain Conway, Sergeant Cohen, and Second Lieutenant Hastings stood before the orderly room door just as the sun made its hesitant appearance on the horizon and the First Squad of the Second Platoon sat their mounts a short distance away.

Conway checked his personnel roster one last time before shoving it carefully into his saddlebags and turning to the men standing just behind him. "As both of you know, what I'm doing is in direct violation of military directives, which state that at no time shall both the commanding officer and executive officer be absent from the post during the same interval, but I'm damned sick and tired of our people getting the short end of the stick. It looks like Lieutenant Kincaid is going to be gone longer than I had anticipated and my command is now six days overdue for pay call and I'll not tolerate any more of this."

Conway paused to take in the young lieutenant, who might well have had the first shave of his life that morning.

"Lieutenant Hastings, you are in command until I get back. Do not hesitate to ask for and accept Sergeant Cohen's advice on any matter of significance that might arise. Sergeant Cohen is of the first rank and there is not a better soldier in the service. While I have no doubt you are a fine officer, you are no better than the noncoms who serve under you. It is a wise man who knows how much he does not know."

"I understand, sir. Things will be properly taken care of here, and good luck with your dealings at Regiment."

"Thank you, Lieutenant," Conway said as he raised boot to stirrup and swung into the saddle before looking down at his first sergeant.

"Have a good trip, sir," Cohen said, saluting smartly.

Conway returned the salute with a snap of his wrist and turned his immaculately groomed bay toward the main gate. Second Squad, in a column of twos, moved out smartly behind him and they were gone before the sun surged into the sky as a prelude to another scorching day.

The four-hour ride to regimental headquarters was a pleasant diversion for Captain Conway. It felt good to have a spirited mount between his legs again and to be away from humdrum affairs of life at Outpost Number Nine. But when they approached the main gates of the regimental fort, the anger that had brought him there returned and he stiffened in the saddle to a textbook image of what an officer in the field was supposed to look like.

Conway returned the guard's salute at the main gate as they entered the fort and cantered toward the stable area, but it was strictly a reflex action, as his mind was given to the task at hand. While his outward demeanor was that of a mounted infantry officer arriving on a routine business call, inwardly he was seething with rage that he should have to ride to headquarters and plead for pay for men who were paid precious little in the first place—when they did get paid.

Conway stepped down with fluid grace and handed his reins to a private on stable duty before turning to Corporal Wilson and saying, "See that the horses are watered and properly cared for, then arrange for your squad to be fed. I don't know how long this is going to take, but we'll by God get a meal out of it if nothing else."

"Yes sir. Squaaaaad, disssmounttt!"

As he walked toward the headquarters building with aggressive strides, Conway worked the gloves off his hands and slapped the dust from his shirt front before sliding the gloves through his weapons belt and letting them hang there in a fold. The solid thud of his boots on the wooden porch fronting the building sent an echo across the silent parade, and when he pushed the door aside it slammed against the wall with a bang.

A startled clerk looked up from his ledger and rose quickly from his chair when he saw the captain.

"May I help you, sir?"

"No, you can't. I want to see the regimental paymaster."

"I'm sorry, sir, but Major Abrahams doesn't wish to have any visitors just now. May I say who is calling?"

"No, and I don't care who the major wishes to see, and don't bother telling him I'm here. I'll tell him myself."

With those words, Conway pushed through the waist-high swinging gates joining the two counters and ignored the clerk's protestation.

"I'm sorry, sir, but you can't just—"

"Don't be sorry, be quiet. And don't tell me what I can and can't do. I'll decide that for myself."

"Yessir," the corporal said as he sank into his chair again with an awed look at the captain.

White lettering painted in an arch on a glass panel in the closed door proclaimed the domain of the regimental paymaster, and Conway rattled the glass with two sharp raps on the wooden panel before pushing the door open without waiting for a response from inside.

A plump, bespectacled, balding man sat behind the desk

with his feet hooked over one corner, a corned-beef sandwich in one hand and a nickel novel spread across disproportionately large thighs. Fleshy jowls quivered as his head snapped toward the sound of the opening door, and words of protest formed around the bread and meat being pulverized within his mouth.

"What . . . what's the meaning of this, . . . Captain? I left specific instructions with Corporal Slade that—"

"Excuse me, Major, but I didn't ride thirty miles to wait out front while you finish your lunch and improve your education. You know me from previous unannounced visits like this, but I'll observe the formality of cordiality anyway. I'm Captain Warner Conway, commanding officer, Easy Company, Outpost Number Nine, and I'm here to by Christ find out why in hell my men haven't been paid."

The major's feet dropped to the floor and he hastily shoved the pulp novel into a desk drawer while placing his sandwich on a napkin. He brushed some errant crumbs from his bulging stomach and lap while swiveling his chair to face the captain.

"Yes, I remember you, Captain," Major Abrahams said in a less-than-pleasant voice. "Won't you please have a seat?"

Conway propped a dust-covered boot on one of the wooden chairs arranged before the desk while pushing the hat back on his head. "I haven't got time to sit, but I've sure as hell got time to listen. Now, why in the goddamned hell hasn't Easy Company received its payroll?"

"Well, Captain, there are many regulations that must be contended with," Abrahams said, clearing his throat and grasping a pencil as though it were a lance to protect him from the irate captain. "Unfortunately, it seems your people out at—what is it? Outpost Number Nine, if memory serves?"

"Memory serves."

"As I was saying, there are many regulations that must be observed—"

"Shove your goddamned regulations. Why the hell haven't my men been paid this month?"

Abrahams smiled with a mixture of concern and superiority. "I'm afraid you're forgetting a slight matter of rank here. I'll not be talked to like some private shoveling dung—"

"That's exactly where you should be, Major, if you can't do your job any better than you have. And I couldn't give less of a damn about your rank. I am in command of a mounted cavalry unit in the field. Our casualties are high and our morale low, especially when we don't get paid. Just about everybody in my outfit is overage in rank, we can't get the supplies we need, our rifles are outdated, and we're under strength, but still we are expected to do a job. And we do a damned fine one. It seems to me if you've got time to sit here on your ass and eat sandwiches and read books, you sure as hell should have time to make out the necessary pay vouchers once a month."

Abrahams pushed his glasses back onto the bridge of his nose and cleared his throat once again. "It's not a simple matter of time, Captain, please be assured of that. It is a matter of regulations."

"Regulations! When it's time for my troops to go up against Mr. Lo and put their lives on the line, they don't sit back and dig out a pile of goddamned regulations and try to find some fine-print reason why they shouldn't do it!"

"Mr. . . . who?"

"Forget it. Obviously he's not a concern of yours anyway. Now, in plain and simple English, why the hell haven't my troops been paid?"

"Basically, Captain, I would say it's your fault," Abrahams answered with a pleased grin of superiority.

"My fault? You'd better explain that, Major, and explain it good," Conway said, advancing on the desk with white-knuckled fists clenched into menacing clubs. "My men come first with me, and no fat-assed paymaster is going to say different and I don't give a shit if you're a goddamned general!"

Abrahams lurched back abruptly in his chair and his glasses slipped again, but he ignored them in his fright. "Now hold on, Captain. Just hold on a minute. This is simply a matter of not following regulations, certainly no overt attempt on your part to shortchange your command."

"You're goddamned right it isn't! Explain, Major. Make it quick and make it good. Right now I couldn't think of a better reason for being drummed out of the service than for busting your face wide open."

"Just hold your temper, Captain. Excuse me while I get the records," Abrahams said with a wary eye on Conway, while sliding out of his chair like an eel, his soft belly drooping down past his belt buckle. "It will only take a moment."

Conway stalked to the window and threw the drawn curtain

aside and looked out at nothing while the major dug in his files.

"Ah, here it is. Easy Company," Abrahams said, squeezing into his chair once more and opening the paybook before him on the desk. He adjusted his glasses with one hand while running his finger down a column with the other. "Yes, yes, here it is. Just as I remembered. The infraction occurred last month, as a matter of fact."

Conway let the curtain fall and crossed the room with angry strides. "Infraction? What infraction?"

"Well, it seems your executive officer, a Lieutenant Matthew Kincaid, signed the paybook last month instead of yourself."

"So? What the hell's wrong with that? It's perfectly legal and in keeping with your precious regulations."

Abrahams allowed a tidy smile to spread apart his bulbous lips. "Yes, Captain, it is. But that is not the point in question here. You see, he signed it where it plainly says, 'Captain and Commanding Officer,' not where it says 'Other,' as he should have. That, Captain Conway, is clearly a violation and your outfit has been red-lined for a month in keeping with regulation number C-487 . . ."

Conway jerked the paybook toward him and turned it to where he could read the previous month's signatures. After he had read them he pushed the book away and slammed his open palms onto the polished wood in disgust. "And you're holding up the pay for my men because of that?"

"Regulations are written to be followed. You should know that, Captain. I didn't write them, but I *do* follow them."

"To the letter, obviously. That is ridiculous, Major. Stupid, asinine, and ridiculous! I've got a mind to drag you out from behind that desk and—"

The door swung open and Lieutenant Colonel Dawson stepped inside with a curious glance at the two men face to face across the desk. "Am I interrupting something, gentlemen?" he asked.

Captain Conway straightened and saluted, and Dawson returned the salute perfunctorily. "How are you, Warner?" the regimental commander asked cordially as he offered his hand.

Conway returned the handshake enthusiastically. "Fine, sir. With the exception of having to deal with the most persnickity son of a bitch in the entire army."

"You wouldn't be referring to our Major Abrahams here, would you by any chance?"

"One and the same," Conway replied, turning to glower at the man behind the desk.

Words of protest caused Abrahams' double chin to jiggle. "You know, Colonel Dawson, sir, how dedicated I am to my job. The regulations were made for everyone to follow. Including Captain Conway there," he concluded hotly.

Dawson's eyes became serious and he turned to the man whom he considered to be his best commanding officer in the field. "What seems to be the problem, Warner?"

"My men haven't been paid this month, sir."

"They haven't? Why not?"

"Because Lieutenant Kincaid signed last month's paybook on the wrong line."

"You're joking."

"I wish I were."

"I know Lieutenant Kincaid, and in my view Matt's one of the most capable young officers in the entire regiment. If he made an error, it would simply have to be an oversight."

"My sentiments exactly, sir," Conway said, his angry eyes drifting to Abrahams' face.

"However innocent the error might have been, Captain, it is still an error and is in violation of regulation numb—"

Dawson stepped forward and snatched a pen from the desk. "We know, Major. We are all painfully aware of how sacrosanct your precious regulations are to you, but they were not written by the right hand of God, as you seem to believe. In matters as simple as this, there is more than enough room for accommodation. Now, where do I sign to override the lieutenant's signature and relegate this mess to the trashcan where it belongs and get Easy Company back on the pay roster where it belongs?"

Abrahams cleared his throat, adjusted his glasses unnecessarily, and shifted uneasily in his chair. "Begging your pardon, Colonel, sir," he began cautiously, "I'm not sure you have the authority to—"

"Major Abrahams! I have sufficient authority to have your ass thrown in the stockade for insubordination," Colonel Dawson said with deadly sincerity. "Which is exactly what I'll do if I hear the word 'regulations' come from your mouth one more time. Now, where the hell do I sign?"

Abrahams' pudgy fingers stabbed quickly at a spot on the lower portion of the page. "I think your initials right here beside the lieutenant's would be sufficient, sir."

"That's more like it," Dawson growled as he scrawled his initials across the bottom of the page and shoved the book back to Abrahams with an icy stare. "These men are part of a fighting unit in the field, Major, where people bleed real blood and often die. Combat is part of their daily existence. They shouldn't have to fight for their pay as well."

"I'm only doing my job, sir," Abrahams said weakly.

"And too damned well at times, I suspect. Good day, Major," Dawson said, turning away and ignoring the major's hasty scramble to his feet and artless attempt at saluting. "Join me in a cup of coffee, Warner?"

"Thank you, sir," Conway replied before looking toward Abrahams once again. "When do I pick up the pay vouchers for my men?"

"Come back in an hour, Captain. They will be ready when you return."

"Thanks so much for your cooperation, Major."

As they walked toward the officers' quarters, Colonel Dawson shook his head and said with a chuckle, "I don't know where the army gets fellows like that, Warner. There must be some secret chamber buried in a mountain somewhere, where bureaucrats like Abrahams are entombed until they have lost all familiarity with the human race and emerge totally devoid of all common logic and compassion for their fellowman."

Conway laughed easily. "I agree with you, sir. And, if that happens to be the case, I'm sure Abrahams must have graduated at the head of his class."

"Without a doubt. To hell with coffee, that was just for the major's benefit. How 'bout a drink in my quarters?"

"Beats the hell out of coffee. Lead the way, Colonel."

eleven

The small fire was built at the base of a naked cliff, upon which dark shadows danced and played to the muted concert of snapping twigs and crackling dry brush. Three braves squatted near the flames and tore hungrily at strips of dried antelope, washing them down with long, thirsty drinks from earthen jugs filled with cool spring water.

Eagle Flies Alone watched them in silence, as did the other Arapaho warriors until the one named Running Wolf took a final drink from the jug and said, "We have not eaten or drunk all day. We waited a long time for the blue-shirts to come."

"Where are our brothers, Lame Crow and the others?" Eagle Flies Alone asked.

Running Wolf glanced once at him, then looked away. "They are dead."

"And the Americans?"

"Two of them are dead as well, maybe three."

"Maybe three?" Eagle Flies Alone snarled, snapping a twig in his hands viciously and throwing it onto the fire. "Six Arapaho warriors for three Americans? You are a disgrace, Running Wolf. Is their leader dead, and the sly one named Mandalian?"

There was pain in Running Wolf's voice when he answered. "No, my brother, they are not. They couldn't have known we were waiting for them at Three Trees, but the sly one should be named for the reptiles. They surprised us with their horses running hard and well-spaced, and by the time we could react, the snake called Mandalian was gone."

"Surprised you?" Lone Eagle asked incredulously. "You were the ones waiting in ambush, not them."

"I know, my brother, but they were upon us so quickly, and the leader of the blue-shirts was not in front as we expected. It was the snake, and as a horseman, he is a match for any warrior here. He was gone before we knew it. Two of our braves went after him." Running Wolf looked up slowly. "They never returned."

"And the leader of the Americans?"

"He was in the rear. The three we killed were in the middle."

Eagle Flies Alone rose and circled the fire and his face was dark with anger. He was deeply engrossed in thought, and the others held their silence, waiting for him to speak again.

"Unless we can trap them, those who survived Three Trees will be at the agency with the others tomorrow. It would have been easier if their leader were dead and that fool I challenged today were in charge, but since he isn't, now we will have to kill him with the others."

Another warrior, Spotted Hawk, looked up from the fire and asked, "Why is the agency so important to us, Eagle Flies Alone? It's only buildings. Why don't we go on to the plains and take what is ours?"

Eagle Flies Alone spun on his moccasined heel, and firelight glinted off his dark eyes. "Because the agency is the symbol of defeat for our people. As long as it stands, they will depend on the white man for their survival. It is easy for them to beg for food and clothing now, where once they would have scoffed at such things. When the agency is gone, they will have no choice but to join us and make war to take back our land."

He paused and his eyes hardened with resolve. "And now everyone at the agency must die. We have taken American lives in violation of the squaw treaty our fathers signed. If there are any survivors left to tell of this attack, we will be hunted by every blue-shirt until we are found and killed. Hear me, we are not strong enough yet to fight them, but when the rest of our people join us—the Crow, the Sioux, the Cheyenne, and our Arapaho brethren, we will again have power to drive them from our land."

Eagle Flies Alone stooped and snatched a jug from the ground and drank deeply before throwing it against the granite wall with a thumping crash. Water ran down his jaw and glistened on his chest as he turned and looked slowly around the fire at the silent warriors.

"Heya, we are in this fight to the death. We are the last hope of the Arapaho people. We are the only ones with courage enough to fight and lead our people back to the way things were in the Grandfather Times. And I don't mean in the same way that that old fool, Gray Bear, means. I will be the new war chief of the Arapaho tribe, and I will lead our people back to the way things really were in the Grandfather Times. We will raid the Utes, we will make war, we will hunt, and we will count coup on anyone foolish enough to trespass on our lands! I have spoken!"

The young warriors surrounding him shouted their approval, and their bronzed faces gleamed in the firelight with hope and the thrill of imminent victory. Eagle Flies Alone watched them with a confident, pleased smile and knew he had done what any great leader and orator had to do. He had brought his warriors back from the brink of despair and prepared them for the coming battle.

When the others were quiet, he moved back into the circle of light once again. "Spotted Hawk, you and two others go to Three Trees tonight and bring our dead brothers back here for burial. Broken Nose? You and Little Smoke go to the mountains where the visions are seen, and find Gray Bear and bring him to me. He must be silenced before he turns more Arapaho warriors into squaws and further deceives our people with his dreams of peace with the white man. When all of you have returned, we will attack the agency."

Eagle Flies Alone paused and looked at his followers, one brave at a time. Then his muscles tensed and he raised his right arm to the sky and his words reverberated off the wall behind them.

"Death to the Americans!"

The other warriors leaped to their feet and raised their right arms in a similar manner and their wild screams echoed across the plains.

"Death to the Americans!"

Eagle Flies Alone watched them with a triumphant sneer crossing his face. Then he turned and stalked away into the night.

The first light of dawn had barely touched the treetops when Matt Kincaid and Windy Mandalian led their ragged group of survivors across the meadow and away from the disaster that had been known as Three Trees. Two soldiers, stiff in death and wrapped in gray blankets, were draped across the backs of their horses and their heads and feet bobbed silently with each step. A third soldier lay strapped to a travois, his eyes closed and teeth gritted against the pain that tore through him each time the crude device bounced across the uneven ground.

At midmorning they were halfway back to the agency, and

Kincaid reined in his horse and waited for the travois to catch up, then moved forward in pace with the pulling horse.

"How are you doing, Pappas?" he asked, looking down at the pale and drawn face of the wounded soldier.

Pappas opened his eyes and looked up. "About as well as can be expected, sir."

"How's the leg?"

"It hurts a mite, but the bleeding hasn't started again, I don't think."

"That's good. I don't want to use that tourniquet again unless we absolutely have to. Leave the damned thing on there too long and you'll lose that leg."

Pappas grimaced and closed his eyes again. "I know, sir. And that's the last thing I want."

"I imagine so. Just hang on for a while longer. We'll be back at the agency in a few more hours."

Pappas only nodded and Matt knew it hurt too much to talk. He reined his horse away and moved up beside Windy again.

"How's he doin'?" the scout asked.

"Fair. Sure hate to lose him now."

"Yeah, we've got enough graves to dig."

"I'd rather not talk about it. What did you make of that smoke the other day, Windy? It was too heavy to be burning buildings, wasn't it?"

The scout nodded, pursed his lips, and spat. "I'd say so, Matt. There ain't enough buildings anywhere roundabouts to cloud up the sky like that."

"Then what do you think the source was?"

"I saw that happen once before, about five years back, up in the Dakotas. The Sioux were burning their land."

"What for?"

"You ever been through where there was a fire, then come back by about two months later after a couple of good rains?"

Matt thought a moment, shrugged, and shook his head. "No, can't say that I have."

"I have. After a fire, the grass greens up and grows like a farmer's son for some reason. These Indians ain't dumb. They've seen that too, and they burn their land a'purpose because of it."

"You said five years back. If it helps that much, why don't they do it every year?"

"Nope. Don't work that way. It's only done when one of

their medicine men predicts a heavy rainfall in the coming autumn. Them old boys don't miss many times with their predictions." Windy chewed the cut-plug in his jaw momentarily before adding, "Guess if they did they'd be out of a job."

"Why's that?"

"If they burn their land and the rains come too late, they're worse off for grass than they were before. No grass, no feed, no game. Simple as that."

"Then no harm is done by their burning and everybody walks away a winner."

"Yup. Except the medicine man, if it don't cloud up and rain like a cow pissin' on a flat rock."

"Don't think I'd want to be in his shoes," Matt said with a chuckle.

"Moccasins," Windy corrected him, then adjusted the rifle in the bend of his arm and spat at a butterfly sitting on a flower. When he missed he said, "Damn. Gonna have to get the fucking thing re-bored, I guess. You know, Matt, the white man would be smart to learn a few things from these Indians, instead of lookin' down on 'em like a bunch of ignorant savages. They've lived on these plains for nobody knows how long, and know all there is to know about the weather and the way things grow. Just those fires the other day should've told any white man to get his winter wood in early. But no, we're too damned smart to realize how dumb we are."

"That's the way it is, I guess. When you're top dog, or think you are, you haven't got time to listen to anybody else."

"Top dog's just as stuck as the bottom dog when they get hung up, Matt."

At just before noon they were still two miles from the agency, and Matt and the others waited in a dry creekbed while Windy went ahead to scout the terrain before them. Not knowing what had transpired at the agency, they had no desire to ride blindly into another trap. If the Arapaho had gone on the warpath for sure, then the agency might have fallen into their hands, and, knowing there were some survivors from the Three Trees ambush, they would surely lay in wait for them at the agency.

An hour later, Windy returned and there was a concerned look on his face. "They've been under attack all right," he said, stepping down from his saddle and squatting on his haunches.

"How bad does it look, Windy?" Kincaid asked, sinking down also and taking up several tiny pebbles, which he absentmindedly tossed and caught in his hand.

"Can't tell for positive. There's some buildings burned for sure, but the agency itself is still standing. Must of been a pretty good-sized war party to get close enough to do that much damage."

"Are there any reservation Indians coming and going?"

"Nope."

"That's a bad sign."

"Yup."

"How about any of our troops?"

"Nope."

Kincaid pondered the pebbles as they rose and fell. "Do you think it's abandoned?"

"Don't think so. There's people there, all right. And whoever it is, they're forted up pretty good."

"If it's the wrong people, going in under a flag of truce won't do a damned bit of good," Matt said, tossing the rocks away. "And if it's our people, a flag of truce wouldn't be necessary."

"I'll ride in alone if you want, Matt. If the hostiles got it, maybe I could lead them away from the rest of you. You sure can't travel fast with poor old Pappas in the shape he's in."

Matt's eyes automatically went to the travois parked in the shade of a cottonwood standing along the bank. "No, we can't. And I want to get him back to the command, where we've got the right medical supplies to treat that wound of his. If it turns to gangrene, he'll lose his leg."

Windy nodded while tearing a fresh chew from the cut of tobacco in his hand. "And if the boys that jumped us yesterday—or their friends—come across him, he'll be just as dead."

"I don't think we've got any choice," Matt said as he stood. "We might as well fight it out at the agency, if it's a fight we've got to have."

They approached the front gate of the agency with their horses moving at a slow walk and fanned out six abreast. The mount pulling the travois was on lead behind them, along with the horses bearing the two dead men, and in the silence the sound of the travois' wooden poles scraping the ground was intensified. They had their rifles across their laps, loaded and at the ready, and they knew not what they were riding into.

When they were still five hundred yards from the main gate, the pounding of running horses swept across the plains, followed by the wild cacophony of yells and screams of a raiding war party. Off to the right, just cresting the rolling swale, twenty warriors raced toward them at a quartering angle.

"They're tryin' to cut us off!" Mandalian yelled.

"Drop those two horses and move out, men!" Kincaid shouted with a sweeping motion of his arm, while the soldier leading the travois shot past them at a dead run. The travois bounced wildly behind the fear-stricken horse pulling it, but Pappas remained lashed to the poles.

The Indians had chosen a path to cut off Kincaid and what remained of First Squad, at an angle that would keep them away from any riflefire coming from the agency but would give them an equal distance to cover. Mandalian, Kincaid, and the four troopers pressed their mounts to a full gallop, staying behind the travois, and they were still three hundred yards from the cutoff point when the Indians, equidistant off to the right, fired their first shots, which went wild.

"Hold your fire till they're closer!" Kincaid yelled, turning his head back toward the four soldiers behind him. More puffs of smoke came from the cluster of ponies at two hundred yards, but still the soldiers held their fire. The travois ahead of them continued to lurch and bounce, but the contraption held together, and as far as Matt could tell, Pappas was still lashed in place.

With no more than one hundred and fifty yards separating them from the Indians now, Kincaid gave the signal to shoot. Simultaneously, six rifles fired, but riflefire from the back of a running horse was bound to be less than accurate, and only one Indian pony went down. Rifles were quickly snapped back onto saddle spiders and revolvers took their places, with the exception of Mandalian, whose Henry held five rounds, one of which slammed into the lead warrior's chest with Windy's second shot.

The Indians continued their random fire, and the soldier just behind Kincaid went down with his tumbling mount. They were catching up with the tiring horse pulling the travois, and Matt knew they would have to slow up to remain abreast of the struggling animal or leave Pappas to a certain death.

Windy looked back, and Kincaid knew that the scout was

thinking the same thing he was, so he screamed, "Do it!"

Mandalian wheeled his horse to the right, as did Kincaid with the soldiers behind following suit, and they rode straight at the closing warriors with revolvers blazing while the travois horse continued on toward the main gate. They were attacking now instead of running, and since it was obvious the Arapahos would have cut them off anyway, they chose to provide the Indians with a frontal target.

Their sudden move surprised the Indians, who had not expected to come under attack while attacking, and several of their horses broke stride as the riders on their backs pulled them up. Off to his left, Kincaid saw several flashes of blue streaking from the main gate, and he fired another shot while saying under his breath, "Easy Company comes a-callin'."

The pursuers were now the pursued, and the warriors spun their mounts on churning hooves and raced away to the left. Two more braves toppled from their ponies before the Indians reached the prairie swell again, and Matt signaled for his men to rein in. Windy jumped from his saddle before his mount had slid to a stop, and quickly dropped to a knee-rest firing position. The Sharps belched flame and another brave toppled over the rear of his horse, just as his companions raced out of range.

"Pretty good shot," Matt observed as he watched the stilled figure lying in the grass.

"Pretty good, my ass," Windy grunted as he stepped up to his saddle. "That was perfect."

Knowing there would be another band of warriors waiting just over the rise, Sergeant Gus Olsen signaled for the squad behind him to quit the pursuit, and they turned their mounts toward Lieutenant Kincaid. Matt glanced back; the trooper whose mount had been hit was up and walking with nothing more than a limp, and Matt turned back to face Sergeant Olsen.

"Welcome home, sir," Olsen said with as much of a grin as his broken mouth would allow.

"Thanks for the help, Sergeant," Kincaid replied as he studied the mass of welts and bruises that had once been a fairly handsome face. "What in the jumped-up Jesus happened to you?"

"Let's just say I ran into a set of knuckles, sir."

"Whose? The entire Third Regiment?"

"Nossir. Just some fellers that we got to know pretty well."

With those words, Kincaid looked at the other members of

the squad; there was not a man among them who wasn't sporting either a black eye, a split lip, or a swollen jaw. "Glad to see Davis is keeping things under control," he said with a shake of his head.

"He's tryin' his best, sir."

"His best doesn't appear to be blue-ribbon material, Sergeant. Thanks again for the help just now."

"We would've been here sooner, but Lieutenant Davis kept insisting that our assignment was to protect the agency."

"That figures."

"When things got to lookin' pretty grim for you, I just couldn't seem to hear him anymore."

Kincaid gazed toward the agency with a look of disgust crossing his face. "I couldn't be more happy for your sudden loss of hearing, Sergeant. There are two mounts back there somewhere, with Cavanaugh and Watson strapped across them. We got jumped and they didn't make it. Round them up and pick up Private Minton on your way back in."

"Yessir."

"We'll be watching in case Mr. Lo decides to take another crack at it."

"Thank you, sir," Olsen said as he cantered away with the squad strung out behind him.

The first thing Kincaid did when he passed through the gates was to turn his horse toward the sweat-drenched and panting animal strapped to the travois and jump down to kneel beside Pappas. The soldier's teeth were clenched together against the pain and his eyes were tightly shut. The blanket over the wounded leg was turning red, and Matt knew the wound had opened again.

"We made it, Ike," he said gently. "You're a tough trooper. Hang on, and we'll get you home as quick as we can."

Pappas' eyes fluttered open. "I appreciate that, sir. That was some ride, I'll have to say that."

"Yeah, I imagine it was. Your wound is bleeding again and I'm going to change dressings and try a compression bandage to see if I can't close it up. If not, we'll have to go to the tourniquet again."

"I can feel the blood, sir, but I don't think I lost too much."

"I hope not. We've come too far to lose you now," Matt said, standing and pointing a finger toward the nearest group of soldiers. "Get this man into the agency and lay him on the counter. Handle him easy, he's hurt pretty bad."

Lieutenant Davis came hurrying across the broad street and snapped to attention with a smart salute, which Kincaid didn't bother to return.

"Glad to see you're back safely, sir," Davis said as his hand slowly dropped from his forehead.

"So am I. What the hell's been going on around here?" Kincaid asked as his gaze swept over the blackened, gutted buildings.

"We've been under attack, sir. We repulsed the enemy but suffered some casualties."

"How many and what kind?"

"Three dead, four wounded."

"Fuck!" Matt said through clenched teeth.

"Pardon me, sir?"

"I said fuck! Didn't they teach you that word at West Point?"

"No, I'm afraid not, sir."

"Well, they should have, because it goes well with 'up,'" Matt said, spinning on his heel and striding toward the agency building, leaving a bewildered Lieutenant Davis standing in the middle of the street.

While Kincaid worked over Pappas' wound, Doug Collins stood beside him and chattered like a squirrel whose nest had just been robbed.

"You wouldn't have believed it, Lieutenant. I have never seen a fight like that, and I doubt you have either."

"Don't be so sure," Matt interjected without looking up.

"There were bodies and blood and furniture and stoves . . ."

"Stoves? You've only got one stove."

Collins continued as though Matt had remained silent, ". . . and the whole kit and kaboodle was scattered around here like cordwood. Animals in a cage would be less inclined to act like that than your men were."

Now Kincaid looked up. "My men? They must have been fighting *with* somebody."

"Oh, sure they were. A bunch of ringtailed range hands who—"

"Hello, Kincaid," Ramsey said from where he stood leaning against the doorjamb. "I didn't know you were a doctor as well as a lover."

Matt's head jerked toward the sound of the voice, and he

saw Ramsey standing there with the Winchester draped casually over his shoulder and an easy smile on his face.

Ignoring the rancher's remark, Kincaid turned back to his work. "Hello, Ramsey. What brings you here?"

"I came to save your army from the heathen. Thought for a minute there I was going to have to save you as well. Nice move, turning the attack on those bastards the way you did."

"Thanks. I've tangled with them a time or two before. You still haven't answered my question. What brings you here?"

Ramsey moved inside and laid his rifle on the counter. "How 'bout a beer, Collins? Kinda hot outside today."

Collins hesitated before stepping around the counter, drawing a beer and thumping it down.

"Put it on my bill," Ramsey said, taking a long drink before turning again to Kincaid. "What brought me here was a bunch of Indians trying to burn the world down. Destroyin' good rangeland and jeopardizing my buildings. We got waylaid by a passel of your friendly, pacified charges. They killed one of my men and you might say this agency here was the only port in a very violent storm. Now I'm gonna hang around and see just what you aim to do about all that."

Matt cinched the last bandage down and patted Pappas' shoulder. "I think we've got the bleeding stopped again, Ike. Just lay there for a while and don't move that leg."

"Thanks, sir. It feels better already."

"Good," Matt said, turning to face the rancher. "There's nothing I can do about your dead rider except catch and prosecute those who killed him, which I intend to do. As far as the fires go, I have no intention of doing anything about that."

"What? You mean you're just going to let 'em get away with it?"

"That's what I mean."

"I don't believe I'm hearin' what I'm hearin'. What the hell is the army for, if not to protect—"

"On which side of the reservation line were those fires set, Mr. Ramsey?"

The young rancher stared at Kincaid for several seconds before glancing down at his beer mug. "Can't tell you that for certain," he said with little enthusiasm. "We were going to check that out when we got jumped."

"I'll lay you five to one they were on the Arapaho side of

the line. And I'll lay you *ten* to one they were set to improve the rangeland upon which the wild game feeds that these Indians depend on for survival."

"Improve the rangeland by burning it away? Come on, Lieutenant, I didn't just fall off the back of a shit wagon."

"Your attitude indicates otherwise, Ramsey, but I'll go to the trouble of filling you in anyway. They burn the grass so that it will grow faster and thicker with the first rains of autumn."

"They *what*? That's the biggest line of bullshit I ever heard," Ramsey said into the glass as he raised it to his lips.

"It's a fact. Ask my scout. He's seen it before."

"I'm not going to ask your scout anything. Those fires were set as a diversion to cover raids on the settlers in this area."

Matt shrugged. "Suit yourself, but leave the Indians alone who set those fires."

Ramsey misinterpreted Matt's direct tone as one of challenge. "And what if I don't?"

"Then you'll have to deal with me," Matt said flatly, and turned to the counter again.

Ramsey watched with a half-smile while Matt began packing up his medical paraphernalia. "Were the Indians who attacked this agency trying to burn it down so a better one would grow with the first rains?"

"No. I'd say there is one more agency here than some of them want right now."

"Some of them, Lieutenant?"

"Yes, *some* of them. The burning of that grass and the observance of age-old traditions, peaceful in nature, indicates to me that the entire Arapaho nation has not gone on the warpath. I'm hoping that what we're dealing with here is a bunch of young bucks out trying to make a name for themselves."

"I think you're right, Matt," Collins said from behind the counter. "Anyway, I certainly hope you are. Did you have any luck finding Gray Bear? He's the only one who can straighten this mess out."

"No. Trying to find an Indian who has lived in those hills all his life is like trying to find a shadow after dark."

Ramsey arched his brows in feigned surprise. "Well now. Doctor, Indian fighter, poet, and lover. You're a real piece of the Lord's work, Lieutenant Kincaid."

Matt closed the satchel with an angry snap of the clasp.

"What's this 'lover' bullshit, Ramsey?" he asked with a cold-eyed stare.

"You know what I'm talking about," Ramsey replied, draining the beer mug and thumping it on the counter. "I take care of my sister, and I don't want anybody messing with her."

"She's a grown woman, Ramsey. She's done nothing against her will."

"Yeah? Well, I think she's done something against *my* will."

"That's your problem," Matt replied, picking up the satchel. "And the Indians who've gone renegade are mine. Now go on back to your ranch and leave army matters to the army to solve."

Ramsey smiled and there was a boyish look of innocence on his handsome face. "Can't do that, Lieutenant, sir. The army's problems are my problems. Me and my men are part of your army now."

"You're what?"

"For a fact, but don't expect me to keep calling you 'sir.' Your Lieutenant Davis sort of deputized us when the ruckus was goin' on. He said we were in the army until he told us different. Something about him representing military law and us being conscripted, if that's the right word."

"Yeah, it's the right word in most cases, but damned awful wrong here. You and your men are officially released from your duties and free to go."

Ramsey shook his head and the smile turned to a leering grin. "Sorry, Kincaid, but I'll have to hear that from the man who said he'd put me in jail if I left. You know I wouldn't want to break any of your precious military laws."

"All right, we'll play the game however you want it. I'll have Davis in here in less than a minute and he'll repeat what I just said," Matt stated flatly as he picked up the satchel and turned to leave. He was halfway to the door when Ramsey spoke again.

"Lieutenant?"

Matt stopped and turned back quickly. "Look, Ramsey, I have neither the time nor the inclination to be involved in your little game."

"This is no game. I saw you hauling two dead men in here today. Three more were waiting for you. This man here isn't worth a damn in a scrap"—he indicated Pappas with an indifferent wave of his hand—"and you've got four more in damned near as bad shape. That's twelve men gone from your command, for all intents and purposes. You're pretty well shot up for takin' on Christ knows how many well-armed redskins, but I'd guess there's upwards of forty. Think about it."

"I've thought about it. We'll get by, we always do."

Ramsey picked up his Winchester and studied it before slowly turning his head toward Kincaid. "This is a Winchester, Model Seventy-seven. It's the newest gun in the West and easily the finest weapon ever made. I can fire six shots with this before you can fire two with those antique Springfields. I've got seven damned good men with me, and counting myself, that makes eight. Each of them is armed with a Winchester just like this one, and with this rifle we're equal to sixteen or more of your soldiers armed with single-shots. Like it or not, Kincaid, you need us bad." Ramsey laid the weapon carefully on the counter. "Like I said, think about it."

Matt glanced at the rifle with its gleaming blue metal, its varnished stock and lever action, and he couldn't help feeling a twinge of envy. He remembered how hard he and Captain Conway had worked to get the company armed with repeating, five-shot Spencers to replace the old single-shot Springfield. And what really galled him as he stood there was the fact that he knew most of the rebel warriors opposing them were armed with Spencers that were probably taken at the Battle of the Little Big Horn and supposedly turned in with the signing of the treaty.

"I won't deny I could use more firepower," he said, his gaze going back to Ramsey. "But you and your men, however well armed, aren't worth a tinker's damn to me if you won't listen to orders."

Ramsey grinned again. "I *listen* to 'em," he said with meaningful emphasis.

"Listen to them, *hear* them, and *carry them out* exactly as given."

"I'm not too awful good at following orders, but my men are. They'll do whatever I tell them."

"They'll do as *I* tell them, and that includes you, or you can get on your donkey and ride."

"You drive a hard bargain, Kincaid, but you've got a deal."

Matt's eyes narrowed as he studied the rancher. "Why? Why do you want to get involved in this?"

The easy smile faded from Ramsey's lips and his face turned hard. "Let's just say I've got a personal interest in your future and an old score to settle with some featherheads."

"My future is not your concern in any regard, and I haven't got any use for men who're out to settle personal vendettas. You do it my way or not at all."

Ramsey shrugged. "Like I said, you've got a deal."

"Fine. I could use the help, and thanks for the offer."

"My pleasure."

Matt turned away and saw Windy standing in the doorway and cradling the Sharps in the crook of his left arm. His eyes were riveted to Ramsey's face, but he spoke to Kincaid.

"Havin' a problem with this feller, Matt?" he asked in a casual tone.

"No, Windy. Nothing I can't handle."

"Didn't figger so. Got a minute to talk?"

"Sure. Walk with me to the stable so I can put this medicine kit away," Matt said, stepping through the doorway.

Windy gave Ramsey one last hard look, then turned and stepped out in stride with Kincaid.

"I've been palaverin' with an old squaw who speaks Cheyenne, and I think I know what Gray Bear was talkin' about, with that 'green arrows as far as the eye can see' line of shit."

"Just a minute, Windy," Matt said, seeing Lieutenant Davis. "Lieutenant Davis!"

Davis was inspecting a rifle and his head jerked up at the sound of his name. Seeing who had called him, he handed the Springfield back to the luckless soldier who was being inspected and hurried to the center of the street.

"Yessir?"

"First of all, what the hell are you doing?"

"Inspecting a rifle, sir."

"Why?"

"Because it looked dirty to me, sir."

"Every goddamned weapon we've got is dirty, Lieutenant. In case you haven't noticed, we are in the field on a combat patrol, not standing parade inspection back at the post. These men are seasoned veterans with more skirmishes under their belt than you've got teeth. They know their lives depend on the performance of their weapons and they'll keep them in firing order. I don't want them harassed about a bunch of nitpicky bullshit. Is that understood?"

"Yessir."

"Good. Now pick a detail and have our dead buried within

the hour. Anywhere outside the agency will do. I want them buried with the maximum military honors we can provide under the circumstances. Have a squad standing by both for your protection and to fire a salute when we perform the ceremony. Have the flag over the agency lowered to half-staff, and tell McBride to be ready to play taps, even though he can't play worth a shit. I'll want the whole company assembled and standing at attention, with the exception of the guard mount. Come and find me when you're ready."

"Yessir," Davis said, snapping a smart salute.

Matt returned the salute and walked toward the stable once more.

"You're bein' just a little rough with the young pup, ain't you, Matt?"

"No more than he deserves. The biggest part of being an officer is being just a little smarter and more practical than the people under you. Davis is still pissin' West Point water and hasn't figured that out yet. Go ahead, what did you learn from that squaw?"

As was his custom, Windy chewed, thought, and spat before answering. "The thing that was supposed to've started this whole shebang was Gray Bear's words about—let me see now if I can get this right—'new green arrows, as far as the eye can see; arrows from Great Turtle, who wants us to live in the ways of the Grandfather Times.' Ain't that right?"

"Yeah. That's what brought us here. What about it?"

"And that's what makes everybody think they're goin' back on the warpath again, right?"

"That's the only interpretation we've had."

"Well, that's bullshit, Matt. Pure and simple."

"What's it supposed to mean, then?"

"You know those fires we were talkin' about?"

"I remember."

"Well, that's where the new green arrows come from."

"You mean they're not talking about war arrows?"

"No. They're talkin' about *grass*. New, tall grass from horizon to horizon."

They were at the stable now, and Matt stowed the medicine kit away in a packsaddle while asking, "And who is this Great Turtle?"

"He's their god of the seasons. Seems like he's promised early rains and that's why they're burning their land. Gray Bear's supposed to have figgered all that out."

"Fine, but then what's this business about returning to the ways of the Grandfather Times? It wasn't too long ago that they were making war on the white man."

Windy spat again. "And rightly so, I figger. But what you just said is exactly what Gray Bear meant. The Grandfather Times were before the white man came. The new grass means plentiful game, and they will hunt on their land and live in peace like they did before we took their land away from them."

"Then you think Eagle Flies Alone has misinterpreted the old man's meaning?"

"Hell, no. And if he did, it's deliberate. I think he's using Gray Bear's words to whip a bunch of young bucks into a frenzy."

"Then we're right in thinking this is not a full-scale uprising, and we're dealing with maybe half a hundred or so warriors instead of an entire nation."

"That's the way I see it," Windy agreed, scratching his bewhiskered jaw. "But if Eagle Flies Alone succeeds with what he's tryin' to do, it's hard to say which way the rest of his people will turn. There's a lot of 'em who ain't too fond of reservation life, and a major victory here just might get 'em riled up again."

Matt closed the last buckle on the packsaddle and stood again. "What do you think the next move will be?"

"That's anybody's guess, Matt," the scout replied, running a hand across the nape of his neck, "but I think Eagle Flies Alone wants the agency real bad, and he'll most likely try to take it again this afternoon. That way, if he's beaten back, he can come back after dark and collect his wounded and dead."

"That's pretty much what I was thinking. He's well armed, and if he can get close enough to use his fire arrows effectively, he's got a damned good chance of burning this place to the ground. If they strike this evening and we beat them back, tomorrow we'll take the battle to them."

"We got no choice, the way I see it. We sure can't bring him to his knees from behind these walls," Windy replied as they moved toward the doorway again.

"Why do you think that old squaw was so cooperative in telling you about the meaning of Gray Bear's words, Windy?" Matt asked when they stepped into the sunlight. "I don't imagine she's any more above a good old-fashioned lie than the rest of them."

A hard look came into Windy's eyes. "In most cases she

wouldn't be. But she has a damned good reason for telling the truth this time. Eagle Flies Alone ran over her son during the attack yesterday. The boy is dead."

Matt took in a deep breath and exhaled slowly. "We've got to stop him, Windy."

Windy turned his head away and spat. "We'll get him. If not tonight, then tomorrow for sure."

twelve

There was a haunting loneliness about the sound of the single bugle crying its mournful salute, which drifted across the vast prairie and was swallowed in the emptiness of the rolling hills. Even though not played to perfection, the melody of taps evoked a tragic sense of loss, of death, of a comrade fallen never to rise again.

When Reb McBride finally lowered his instrument, the five bodies were lowered into freshly dug graves and the gray of the blankets covering them was but a shade lighter than the rich prairie sod. Upon Matt's command, eight rifles fired as a single weapon and the echo of their rattling blast was a finalizing sound that eradicated the bugle's call from the stilled air.

"All right, Lieutenant Davis," Kincaid said, replacing the hat on his head and turning to the officer beside him, "dismiss the platoon and have them return to battle positions. You stay here with the burial detail until the graves are closed, and keep a squad here for your protection."

"Yessir."

Matt returned the lieutenant's crisp salute and walked beside Windy back to the agency compound. "I can't ever get over the feeling that comes with seeing my men, good, brave men, buried so far away from families and friends. The feeling of loss is overwhelming, and I'll have to admit I sometimes wonder if it's all worth it."

"It's that goddamned song you play, Matt," Windy said, reaching for his plug of tobacco and tearing off a chunk now that the service was over. "Seems to me like you could've picked a little bit more cheerful tune. That's the most mournful son of a bitch I ever heard."

"Taps?" Kincaid asked with a weak smile. "Old army tradition. I don't think a snappy Irish jig would be quite appropriate."

"Maybe not, but dead's dead, and a grave's a grave, no

matter where the hole is dug. And a miserable song like that don't help matters a damned bit."

"No, I suppose not."

Collins saw them just as they stepped inside the gates, and he hurried in their direction with three elderly Arapaho following him at a more cautious pace.

"Matt," Collins called out as they neared, "these three men are here as representatives of their tribe. They are all chiefs from the various bands and each of them was a signatory to the truce. Their spokesman is Red Wing, the one in the center, and they have come to assure you that the Arapaho nation as a whole is not involved in this uprising." Collins hesitated with a glance at the three expressionless Indians now standing behind him. Then he added in a lowered voice, as though revealing a secret, "Also, Red Wing is Eagle Flies Alone's father."

Matt stepped forward and offered his hand, shaking with each of the chiefs in turn. "Thank you for coming. My name is Lieutenant Kincaid, this is Windy Mandalian."

Windy nodded and the chiefs returned the gesture. Each of them was dressed in traditional Arapaho clothing, with vests and pants of tanned hide, chest pieces made of interlocking bones, and all three had twin eagle feathers in their black hair as marks of their rank.

Red Wing held his silence momentarily, and when he spoke there was a halting slowness to his words, as if time and travail had stolen his strength from him. But his eyes told a different story. There was a brightness about them and a depth that bespoke wisdom. He looked directly at Matt and his unblinking gaze never faltered.

"Hear me, we are here as representatives of the Arapaho people. We do not wish to make war with the white man and desire only to live in peace. We signed a treaty with you in good faith and we have not broken our word, even though Wah-shah-tung does not send all the food and supplies he has promised us. It is the young who wear the warpaint because they have not the patience nor the wisdom to listen to our counsel. They are led by my son, Eagle Flies Alone, and he is the one to blame. The others have been deceived by him."

"Thank you, Red Wing," Matt said with sincerity. "I do not wish to punish all the Arapaho people for the misguided actions of a few. Your son, and those who follow him, will be captured and punished. Many have died on both sides and that is a tragedy. I apologize for my government's not having provided you with the things promised, and I will have my chief, Captain Conway, submit your complaint immediately upon my arrival back at the outpost."

"Thank you, Lieutenant," Red Wing said as he folded his arms across his chest. "You are a man of honor. We have seen much war and suffered much heartache, my people, and we want to see no more young braves die in a struggle they cannot win. We burn the grass to enrich the land for wild game, and we want only to live out our lives in peace."

Matt nodded and offered his hand again. "And that you shall, Red Wing. You too are a man of honor and I trust your word. Return to your people now, and tell them that only the guilty will be punished. We too wish only to live in peace with the proud Arapaho."

The chiefs again returned the handshake, then turned without a word and walked toward their ponies and swung gracefully onto their blanketed backs. And when they rode from the agency, there was a sense of dignity about them; clearly they were not beaten, only suppressed.

"I'm not sure that what we've done is right, Windy," Matt said as he watched the chiefs until they were out of sight. "This land was theirs for centuries, and we have taken it from them in the name of progress."

"Can't be helped, Matt. There are more people coming West every day, and your job is to protect them."

"Protect Ramsey and persecute Red Wing? An unfair trade at best." Kincaid looked at Collins. "Doug, I want you to make out a list of grievances for me to take back to Captain Conway. Whatever you need that you haven't got, I want to know about. I want these people supplied as they were promised in the treaty, and I'll do my damnedest to make sure that they are."

"Sure, Matt. Be glad to. But it's gonna be one hell of a long list."

"Fine. Don't leave anything out. Tell Ramsey I want to see him and to wait for me in the agency. When Davis gets through, we're going to have a meeting and discuss some strategy. Windy, Davis, myself, and the platoon sergeant will be there within the half-hour."

Collins shook his head in disgust. "Ramsey won't be hard to find, Matt. As long as there's any liquor left in the agency to drink, he'll be in there drinkin' it."

"Matt?" Windy said, stepping up beside the officer. "I don't think I'd add too awful much to your meeting. What say I ride out and look around a little bit? Maybe I can get a line on where Eagle Flies Alone is holed up. Could come in handy tomorrow."

"Sure, Windy, but be careful. They should be on the prowl before too long if our hunch is correct."

Windy grinned. "While I ain't claimin' it's too awful purty, I am kinda fond of this hair. Think I'll keep it a while longer."

When they gathered in the agency building a half-hour later, Ramsey stood at the bar drinking beer with the rider Lars by his side. Matt stepped into the building, followed by Davis and Gus Olsen. Lars's battered face was easily a match for the platoon sergeant's, and they nodded cordially, with no hint of animosity.

Matt looked at the rancher closely as he moved to the counter. "Are you going to be sober enough to fight this afternoon, Ramsey?" he asked, waving Collins's offer of a beer aside.

"Since when do you have to be sober to fight, Kincaid? There's not a featherhead out there that I couldn't handle, drunk or sober."

"I think you'll have a chance to prove that before very long."

"I'm waitin'. Set us up another here, barkeep."

While Collins poured the beer, Matt pulled the gloves from his hands and laid them on the counter. "All right, then, here's what it looks like. I think Eagle Flies Alone will attack late this afternoon in hopes of catching us with our guard down. We're going to disappoint him a little bit if he does. Mr. Davis, did they use that rise to the west to cover their approach last time?"

"That's right, sir. They made a frontal attack on the agency while some of them got close enough to use their fire arrows and later scale the walls."

"Then we'll assume they'll do the same thing again. One good thing about Mr. Lo, he seems to have a one-track mind."

"Mr. Lo?" Ramsey asked.

"Yeah. 'Lo,' as in 'Lo, the poor Indian.'"

Ramsey reached for his fresh beer and sloshed some over the side as he jerked the mug to his lips. "They should all be low on their thievin' asses, that's where they should be. What was that powwow about with those three old duffers?"

"They came to profess the innocence of the majority of their people."

"Innocence? There ain't a fucking one of 'em that shouldn't be danglin' at the end of a rope."

"Wrong, Ramsey. Most of them want to live in peace. There's just a few young bucks wanting to make war." Kincaid looked the young rancher straight in the eye. "Rather like yourself, I suspect."

"What's that supposed to mean?"

"They believe that all white men are bad, just as you feel about the Indian. They'd rather fight than talk."

Ramsey grinned into the mug. "Get a hell of a lot more settled that way, Lieutenant. A bullet usually gets a man's undivided attention."

"Tell that to the dead men," Kincaid said flatly. "Now let's get down to business. Ramsey, I want you and your men with those Winchesters on the west wall. You can put up a lot of firepower with those repeaters, and it just might blunt their assault. My troops will cover the east wall and the remainder of the compound, with some men on the walls and some in the buildings on the east side to get a full field of fire. If they make a charge through the compound, only those on the east side will fire. If we shoot from both sides of the street, we'll very likely kill as many of our own people inadvertently as we will the enemy."

Lieutenant Davis looked down and scrubbed the floor with the toe of his boot, wondering why he hadn't thought of that during the first attack.

Kincaid turned to the platoon sergeant. "Sergeant, I want half a squad assigned to blanket detail to put out any fires before they get out of hand. Collins? You be ready to take care of any casualties we might suffer. They'll be brought to the storage shed across the way."

"Why not bring them here, sir?" Davis asked. "This is by far the most secure building."

"Yes, and the one they want most to burn down. If they do manage to get a good blaze going, I don't want any wounded men trapped inside."

"Yessir," Davis replied in a lowered voice, and looked down at the floor again.

Kincaid continued, "They are attacking this late in the day, if they do attack, for two reasons: first, they know we won't pursue them in the dark, even though I'm sure they wish we would; second, they will be able to retrieve their wounded after the sun goes down. If they are seen trying to recover either dead or wounded, I want no shots fired at them. Is that understood?"

"Why not?" Ramsey asked. "Two dead Indians beats the hell out of one."

"Because it's a personal belief of mine. Neither dead nor wounded should be left on the field of battle."

"They wouldn't do that for us."

"Probably not, Ramsey," Matt said icily. "But then, who are supposed to be the heartless heathens? Them or us?"

Ramsey drank his beer in silence, and Matt went on, "Windy Mandalian, my scout, has gone out to see if he can't locate their camp and maybe get a fix on how many warriors we're up against. He should be back in an hour or two. In the meantime I want our forces deployed in the manner described, and prepared for battle. Are there any questions?"

"Yeah, I got a question," Ramsey said. "Why don't we go out and take the bastards on head-to-head, instead of hidin' in here like a bunch of schoolgirls?"

"Because our main responsibility is the protection of this agency. If we beat them back this afternoon, we'll attack in the morning at first light. If we put it to them good enough now, I don't think they'll try a third assault on this compound. Any other questions?"

Matt waited and looked at each silent face in turn until Collins finally spoke up.

"Matt, I ain't much good with blood."

"Get good, Doug. We need all the help we can get. Anything else?"

There was no response and Kincaid said, "Very well, then, let's get to our positions."

The three soldiers moved toward the door, but Ramsey and Lars remained at the counter and slowly nursed their beer. Matt stopped in the doorway and turned around. "That includes you and your man there, Ramsey. Move it out. Now!"

Ramsey shifted his weight from one foot to the other, twirled the mug slowly in his hand, then drained the glass and nodded to Lars. They followed Kincaid, Davis, and Olsen onto the street.

Matt glanced at the lowering sun as he worked his way along the west wall and judged it to be no more than an hour until sunset. A fleeting hope passed through his mind that perhaps they wouldn't be challenged that evening after all, but just then he heard the crackling of gunfire in the distance. His pulse quickened and he turned toward the sound.

"Be ready," Kincaid said to the men nearest him. "I think Windy's gotten himself in a bit of trouble."

A minute passed and the sound of weapons fire drew closer, until a roan horse with a rider wearing buckskins burst over the knoll. The man was huddled low on his horse's neck and firing over the animal's rump with his revolver. The horse was stretched out in a dead run, and even at that distance Matt could see the reddish hide glistening with sweat.

Mandalian was halfway to the main entrance when the first brave topped the crest and pulled his mount in with the others coming up behind in a boiling mass of horseflesh. When he knew the scout would make it safely to the compound, Kincaid hurried to the ladder and stepped quickly down just as Windy's lathered horse pounded onto the street and slid to a grinding stop. Mandalian jumped from his mount and turned the animal into the stable with a slap on the haunch, and the dripping animal bolted inside with a sideways skitter.

"What's it look like, Windy?" Matt asked, crossing the street with long strides.

"I kinda kicked over a hornets' nest, Matt. I found their encampment about five miles from here, alongside the bluffs. I was countin' heads when I got jumped. They were just gettin' ready to head this way and it looks like I hurried 'em up a bit."

"Glad to see you made it. How many warriors do you figure Eagle Flies Alone has?"

"I'd say around fifty or so, give or take a loincloth here and there. They'll be makin' a move on us as soon as they rest their ponies."

"Fifty? I thought Davis said something about thirty or forty."

"Maybe he's a slow counter. Then again, maybe more of them young fellers have joined him."

Matt looked around. "Either way, we're as ready for them

as we're going to get. How about setting up camp in the agency building and keeping an eye on the troops assigned there?"

Mandalian was already moving away. "You'll know where to find me if you need me."

The attack started ten minutes later. Eagle Flies Alone had split his braves into three groups, with approximately twenty mounted warriors breaking over the knoll at the north end of the compound and twenty more pounding over from the south. Ten braves approached on foot to take up prone positions in the grass and shoot at the defenders on the walls, while ten more carried their bows low before them, with pitch-drenched fire arrows notched in place. The two mounted groups hit either end of the street at the same time and they lay low across their horses' necks and fired at the buildings as they raced past with blood-curdling screams. The fire arrows arched high, trailing plumes of smoke into the compound, and the braves on foot dropped to their stomachs and laid a heavy barrage of fire into the upper walls.

The two groups of warriors flashed past each other in opposite directions, and the interchanging silhouettes confused the soldiers in the buildings so that they had difficulty in selecting a target and sticking with it. Due to the heavy fire of the Indians in the grass, the effectiveness of Ramsey's men with their Winchesters was minimized, and they had to snap-shoot, rising to the edge of the wall and firing and then dropping down again.

Matt trained his revolver on a young buck riding a brown and white pinto, and he followed him carefully before squeezing the trigger. The wide-nosed slug slammed home against the warrior's upper abdomen, just below the rib cage, and he lurched upward as he toppled from his horse's back. Several blazes had started as another round of fire arrows sailed into the agency, and Matt looked frantically around for Olsen's fire brigade and saw them dousing flames around the stable door. He could hear the shrill whinny of terrified horses, and he knew the stables had been selected as a primary target by the attacking force.

As quickly as they had come, the mounted warriors were gone to regroup and charge again from opposite directions. Kincaid saw flame tickling the ledge of the agency window, and he thought briefly about Windy, then concentrated on accuracy as the warpainted ponies raced into the compound again at a dead run. He didn't know which of the two lead riders was the renegades' leader, but he fired at both of them with no success.

More fire arrows sailed into the compound, and one soldier straightened on the east wall with a burning arrow in his chest; his clothes were quickly aflame as he toppled over the side and crashed onto the boardwalk below. When the Indians raced away a second time, Kincaid counted five riderless ponies.

Matt took aim on the last rider in the second group; just as he was squeezing the trigger, the brave's horse's knees buckled, its head turned sideways, and it fell heavily on its left shoulder. Its rider was thrown onto the street and knocked unconscious momentarily. By the time he regained his feet, Mandalian was on him with a flying tackle. They rolled over and over before Windy landed a crushing right to the Indian's jaw and he lay still in the thick dust.

Grabbing the brave beneath the arms, Windy backed toward the agency building just as the Indians raced through the compound on their third pass. Another trooper slumped over a window ledge, while a third soldier went down on the agency roof, and four more braves lay sprawled on the street. Several buildings were engulfed in flame and a blaze was spreading across the front of the agency.

But the attack was over. Eagle Flies Alone had suffered all the casualties he could afford, and now he wheeled his mount just out of rifle range with his remaining braves behind him and shook a clenched fist in rage and triumph. Then he was gone, and dusk settled over the compound. The heavy silence was broken only by the crackling of burning timbers.

Kincaid ran toward the agency, grabbed a bucket, and, dipping it into a trough, sloshed water on the blaze. After several repetitions, the flames were out and he tossed the bucket aside. The fire brigade was working on the other buildings, and they managed to save one, but the other two were quickly gutted and their roofs sagged precariously toward the ground. The fire around the stable door was out, and handlers rushed in to calm the excited mounts.

Matt stepped into the agency and saw Windy standing over the still-unconscious Indian, his Sharps mere inches from the warrior's head.

"Thought you might want to have one of these, Matt," he

said dryly, apparently oblivious to the flames that had engulfed the door. "That's why I just shot his horse out from under him."

"Yeah, Windy, good thinking. He might come in handy tomorrow. We'll have to attack in the morning. The compound won't take another raid like that last one."

"There might not be another, the way I see it. They lost quite a few people in that last skirmish. I don't think Eagle Flies Alone can afford the price."

"Neither can we, partner. We lost three more today, and that makes eight dead on what was supposed to have been a peaceful patrol. We'll have to take Eagle Flies Alone on on his own ground and bring an end to this insurrection."

Ramsey burst into the building, his face livid with rage. "Let's go after those bastards, Kincaid! Let's take 'em and take 'em good!"

"Calm down, Ramsey. We—"

"Calm down, your ass! I say we go after 'em!"

"You haven't learned a whole hell of a lot about Indian fightin' yet, have you, son," Windy said without rancor; but it wasn't a question. "There's nothing Eagle Flies Alone would like better than for us to go after him in the twilight. I guarantee you, you'd learn a whole hatful about ambushes."

Frustrated, Ramsey stared at the calm-faced scout, then looked at Kincaid again. "Eddie's lying dead up there on the wall, and Neil's got a bullet through his shoulder, and you tell me to calm down? I want those bastards, and I want 'em dead!"

For the first time, Ramsey saw the Indian lying on the floor. He lunged forward with a boot drawn back to deliver a kick to the man's head, but Windy slammed his Sharps across the young rancher's chest and knocked him off stride.

"You won't be kickin' a man that's down, feller. Not while I'm around," the scout said icily.

Ramsey regained his physical balance and his mental equilibrium at the same time, and looked at both men with something nearing shame in his eyes. "Sorry. Guess I lost my head."

"That's easy to do in battle, Ramsey," Matt said. "This isn't as much fun as you thought it was, is it?"

Ramsey turned and stalked out the door, saying, "I can handle my own, Kincaid. I'll be ready to go when you are."

Matt moved toward the door as well. "Keep an eye on our pal there, will you, Windy? I've got to see how much damage has been done and how many casualties we suffered. Is Collins over at the storage shed taking care of the wounded?"

"He's over there, Matt. That's all I can tell you. Don't worry about young Mr. Lo here. He's never been in better hands."

"That I know. I don't like his chances if he wakes up," Matt said as he stepped outside.

Lieutenant Davis was helping a wounded private into the warehouse, and Kincaid's pace slowed as he saw the arrogant officer with a common enlisted man's arm draped across his shoulders. His attitude toward Davis changed instantly and he said in a deferential tone, "I'd like to see you a minute, Lieutenant, when you get a chance."

Davis craned his neck to see behind the grimacing private. "Not just now, sir. I've got some wounded that need attention."

"That's all right. Take care of your men and find me when you're through," Kincaid said, walking away in search of Sergeant Olsen, whom he found just leaving the stable.

"We're takin' it on the chin pretty good, sir," Olsen said as he approached Kincaid.

"I'm aware of that, but the agency is still intact. Get a detail together and drag those dead warriors out about five hundred yards from the compound. Their friends will come for them sometime during the night."

"Yessir," Olsen replied, but it was obvious there was something else troubling him.

"What's on your mind, Olsen? Let's hear it."

"Well, if you don't mind my askin', sir, how long are we gonna sit here on our asses and let them bastards take potshots at us?"

"No longer. Windy knows where they're camped and we'll take them in the morning. If I can work it out, I'd like to end this thing without any more bloodshed on either side. Eagle Flies Alone knows by now that he can't take the agency, and if he can't destroy this compound, and us, his medicine will start to fail. They've lost quite a few more braves than we have soldiers, and nobody, even an Indian, likes to have the odds against him."

"You mean we'll be in the field again tomorrow, Lieutenant? Mounted and riding to the attack?"

"That's what I mean."

A weary smile broke across the sergeant's weathered face.

"I'm all for that, sir. I'm sick of this stinking place."

"So am I, Sergeant. So am I."

Kincaid crossed to the warehouse and the first man he went to was Pappas, who had been transferred from the agency building. "How are you doing, Ike?" he asked as he laid a hand on the private's shoulder.

"Okay. No more bleedin' just now. That sounded like quite a fight."

"Yeah, it was."

"Sorry I wasn't able to help," Pappas said, looking away. "I heard taps this afternoon. How many have we lost so far?"

"Eight."

Now the wounded man's eyes misted over, and he blinked several times. "Every man in this outfit was my friend. If I quit the service now, it'd be like turning my back on 'em, wouldn't it, sir?"

"Like I said before, Ike, that's your decision to make," Kincaid said with a gentle squeeze of Pappas' shoulder. "You rest now, and I'll see to the others."

Matt turned away but stopped when he heard the softly spoken words, "Lieutenant Kincaid?"

"Yes, Ike?"

"My mind is made up, sir. It's gonna cost me Sarah, but I'll have to take that like a man. I'm going to stay in."

"Be more than pleased to have you, Ike. But you've got a couple more days to think about it. Use them and make your decision when we get back to the post."

Pappas' eyes were closed and his face was drawn tight. "No need for that, sir. My mind's made up. I love her, but I can't let my buddies down."

Matt watched him for several moments, then pursed his lips and nodded his head slowly. "No, Ike. I guess you can't. There aren't many good men who can."

thirteen

The sun was no more than a feeble gray promise on the eastern horizon when Kincaid stepped into the agency building again. Every man in Easy Company who could ride and shoot was mounted and waiting in a column of twos on the wide street. The range hands sat their horses to the rear of the army unit and smoked cigarettes, their legs hooked over saddle horns. Ramsey had dismounted and followed Kincaid into the building.

Windy looked up from where he sat with the Sharps across his lap and scratched his beard while jabbing a thumb toward the sullen-faced Indian bound and propped in the corner.

"He decided to stay the night," the scout said laconically.

"Strictly voluntary, I can see, Windy."

"Wouldn't have it any other way, Matt."

Ramsey moved up beside Kincaid, and there was instant hatred in his eyes when he looked at the Arapaho. "What are you going to do with that bastard, Lieutenant?" he asked. "One bullet in the head would finish the job nicely."

"For you, maybe, but not for me. I'm going to set him free."

"What!"

"You heard me."

The Indian stared at them impassively with a slight sneer curling his lips.

Ramsey shook his head in disgust. "You're gonna let that mother-rapin', hair-liftin' son of a bitch go free?" he asked incredulously.

"That's what I said."

"Well kiss him once on the ass for me, will you?"

"Shut up, Ramsey," Kincaid said, without looking at the rancher, as he moved toward the Indian. "What's your name?"

The warrior stared at Matt in silence before saying, "Wing-foot."

"Wingfoot. Does that mean you can run fast?"

The Indian nodded.

Kincaid squatted on his haunches before the captive. "Well, Wingfoot, I'll tell you what I'm going to do. I don't know how fast you can run, but I intend to find out how fast you can ride. I'm going to let you go. There's a horse waiting for you outside."

Wingfoot watched the officer with wary, untrusting eyes.

"But," Matt continued, "in return I'm going to ask a favor of you. I want you to take a message to your leader, Eagle Flies Alone. Not just now, but when we get close enough so you can't tip our hand. What I want you to tell him is this: he can't win. His own people are against him. Besides, I've sent a messenger back to my post and in two days there will be an entire regiment on its way here to settle this matter, and I don't think they will be in a very understanding mood when they get here. I would like to talk with Eagle Flies Alone under a flag of truce because I don't want to see any more men die, either white or red. He can't take the agency, and without the agency he is nothing. His uprising is over and the only hope he and his braves have is to surrender." Matt stood and looked down at the young brave. "You have an hour to think it over. I hope, for your sake and the sake of your brothers, that you make the right decision," Kincaid concluded, turning to the scout. "Take him to his mount, Windy, and stay with him."

"Sure, Matt," Windy said, patting his rifle and arching a wad of spittle into the top of the stove at the same time. "I don't think he'll be any problem. There ain't a horse or man made yet that can outrun a bullet from this old blunderbuss here."

Kincaid nodded and turned to Collins. "Doug, your store-room and supplies are intact, and I want you to double the rations to any Arapaho who comes for them. We'll be back later in the day."

"Okay, Matt, whatever you say. But I'm gonna need another shipment damned quick."

"You'll get it."

When the platoon moved out, the troopers felt like caged animals set free. They were glad to be on their horses again and moving into battle. Somehow, fighting a defensive war had been alien to their nature and the restrictions of being attacked without attacking had worked a psychological hardship on them. Now they would take Mr. Lo on, face to face, and they were eager with anticipation. Windy rode off to one side with the Indian's reins in his hand, while Matt and Ramsey rode at the head of the column as they moved onto the open prairie with the sun just peeking over the horizon.

Ramsey reined his horse around a boulder, then moved up beside Matt once again. "Let me get this straight," he said. "You think Eagle-whatever-in-hell-his-name-is, is going to just give up without a fight?"

"That's what I think."

"What makes you think that?"

"It's called a bluff, Ramsey. An old poker player like yourself ought to be able to understand it. If I can make him think he's defeated, he will be defeated."

"You mean there's no regiment of troops on its way up here?"

"Nope. I couldn't spare a messenger even if I wanted to, which I don't. His band is shot up pretty good, just like we are. If I can put him in a defensive position, I think he'll have to bargain."

Ramsey shook his head. "I think we should take 'em and be done with it."

"Do you think we *could* take them, Ramsey?" Kincaid asked, turning in his saddle and looking at the troop strung out behind him. "We are less than thirty men, and he must have somewhere between forty and fifty left. The only thing we have in our favor is the threat of more to come. I'm sure Eagle Flies Alone thought he could take the agency, burn it to the ground, and ride away a hero to his followers and to those he wished would follow him. But he didn't plan on us being here, and his scheme hasn't worked and won't work. Even though he has us outnumbered, his back is against the wall. I think he will negotiate."

"And what if he doesn't?"

Matt turned to the rancher and smiled. "Then I guess we'll find out how good a fighter you really are."

When they were a mile from the encampment at the foot of the cliffs, Kincaid signaled for the platoon to halt and waved for Windy to bring Wingfoot forward. There was a different look on the Indian's face now, which revealed a mixture of respect and indecision. He sat the McClellan saddle awkwardly, with his feet free of the stirrups, and it was obvious that he was uncomfortable with what the enlisted men had dubbed "the old nut-buster," pressing against his crotch.

"Now you know what makes us so mean," Kincaid said with a nod toward the saddle.

The Indian's expression became impassive and he watched Kincaid silently with no response.

"All right, Wingfoot," Matt began again, this time in a stern voice, "you're on your own. Tell Eagle Flies Alone that he will be hunted down by every blue-leg in the territory until he is found and killed, if he doesn't accept the offer I'm making. The only chance he has is to meet with me under a flag of truce and discuss the terms of his surrender. Is that understood?"

Wingfoot continued to watch Matt suspiciously, but finally he nodded.

Matt turned to the scout. "Windy? Is there a wide, flat, and open piece of ground near the cliffs?"

"Yep. About a quarter of a mile away to the south."

"Good," Kincaid replied and looked at the Indian again. "Tell Eagle Flies Alone we will be waiting for him there. I will expect him to be there in one hour. If he isn't, we will attack and take no prisoners."

The forcefulness and absolute confidence in Kincaid's voice caused the young Indian's eyes to waver and he looked away as he nodded again.

"Fine. Turn him lose, Windy."

Mandalian handed Wingfoot the reins and the Indian hesitated, certain he would be shot as he rode away.

"Go on, goddammit! Get the hell out of here!" Windy roared and slapped the horse on the rump. "The lieutenant hasn't got all fucking day to wait for you!"

The horse bolted into a gallop and Wingfoot was gone, his bare heels dug into the animal's flanks and his body bent low behind its neck, empty stirrups flapping wildly against the horse's sides.

Matt chuckled as the Indian disappeared over a rolling swale. "Ridin' like that on a nut-buster, I don't think our friend Wingfoot is going to be makin' too many babies."

"I'd buy him a drink just to see him *walk* after a mile of that," Windy added with the laughter of the troops rising behind them.

"Okay, let's get to that rendezvous. I want to be waiting when Eagle Flies Alone gets there."

"Do you really think he'll come, sir?" Davis asked.

"He'll be there, Lieutenant. The hook is baited, now let's see how big a fish we bring in."

The grass was wet with dew and the heat of the rising sun raised the sweet smell of chlorophyll, an odor so thick and musty it could almost be tasted. The greenness of the landscape was broken only by lush fields of wild flowers, and an almost total lack of wind seemed to mute the calling of birds and make even more leisurely the prairie dog's rest, where they sunned themselves by their burrows. And the men of First Platoon, Easy Company, their ranks decimated through death and injury, were spread out across the plains and waiting for, even anxious for, battle.

"How long do you figure we've waited, Windy?" Matt asked from where he, the grizzled scout, and Ramsey sat their horses in front of the platoon.

"Forty-five minutes, maybe. Could be a little more."

Ramsey shifted in his saddle. "They won't be here, Kincaid. They've probably circled around and are knocking the shit out of the agency right now."

"I don't think so, Ramsey. I've offered them a direct challenge and I think Eagle Flies Alone will respond. Saving face is the most important thing to these Arapaho, and he won't want to appear a coward to his warriors, which is how he will be judged if he fails to meet me here. Even the destruction of the agency is not as important to his cause as proving to his people that he is a strong and brave leader."

"Well, I'll have to admit he's got courage," Ramsey said grudgingly. "Riding into the agency three times like he did under all those guns would have to take a dab of guts."

Windy looked around and breathed deeply as a lilting breeze lifted the hair at the nape of his neck. "To protect this land, or win it back, I think any man would have done the same."

A trooper behind them lifted a hand, pointed toward the horizon, and said, "Sir? Looks like we've got company comin'."

Kincaid, Ramsey, Davis, and Windy looked toward the north as one. There they were, spread out across the prairie and riding side by side, their spotted ponies walking slowly as though waltzing to nature's music. They appeared almost mirage-like, and they made no sound. At a distance, their gaudy warpaint made them look like flowers of the plains, and the feathers in their hair and those braided into their horses' manes moved with the breeze.

"I count forty-seven, Matt," Windy said without taking his eyes off the approaching Arapaho.

"That's what I came up with too, Windy. The one in the center at the lead must be Eagle Flies Alone."

All eyes watched the central warrior, whose horse moved straight ahead without any obvious guidance from its rider; he was flanked by two other painted braves.

"We must've had one of his top dogs, Matt," Windy said, his keen eyes picking out details the others could not discern at that distance. "That's Wingfoot on his left."

"Is it? By God, I think you're right."

"I know I am," Windy replied without conceit. "And he's still ridin' your horse, but he must've thrown the saddle away."

"Best thing he could've done," a trooper behind them mumbled.

The bay gelding was more clearly visible now, and it was the only horse approaching them that was of one consistent color. When they were approximately a hundred yards away, the Indian mounts came to a stop and the two opposing forces watched each other in mutual mistrust and hatred. As if perhaps in anticipation, the prairie animals and birds fell silent and nothing moved, with the exception of the occasional switch of a horse's tail.

Kincaid turned and looked down the line of troops before his eyes sought out Lieutenant Davis. "Lieutenant, I'm going out to meet them halfway. Use your own judgment. Be prepared to attack if necessary, but don't react unless the situation deteriorates dramatically. Do you understand that?"

"Yessir sir."

"I hope you do. Our lives are in your hands."

Davis swallowed hard and his sharp Adam's apple bobbed once beneath tight skin. "I understand, sir. There won't be any repeats of what happened the other day."

"That's good enough for me," Matt said, turning toward Windy and Ramsey. "Shall we go out and meet them, gentlemen?"

Windy nodded and Ramsey moved his horse forward without comment. There was a grim, bitter look on the young rancher's face and his features were so sharp and cold he might have been chiseled from stone.

When they had traveled half the distance between the two forces, Kincaid pulled in his mount and waited. Eagle Flies Alone continued to watch them for nearly a minute before his horse moved forward with the two braves by his side. And when they stopped, there was no more than ten yards of open grass between them.

Kincaid's eyes were locked on the young brave in the center as he asked, "Are you Eagle Flies Alone?"

The Indian simply nodded.

"I'm Lieutenant Kincaid, United States Army. You and your braves are under arrest for gross violations of the treaty existing between our two peoples."

Eagle Flies Alone's expression remained impassive, but there was a hint of humor in his words. "I am under arrest, Lieutenant?" he asked as he looked at the line of mounted infantry some fifty yards away. "I would say you and your soldiers will be fortunate to leave here with your lives."

"We are but a few of the many to come. As I'm sure Wingfoot told you, there is an entire regiment on its way here right now. On this day you have more warriors than I have soldiers, but that is only temporary. In the interest of yourself and your people, I am asking for your surrender."

It was obvious, even behind the warrior's blank mask, that the threat of a major campaign was of concern to him, but he asked, "Surrender? Why should I surrender?"

"Because you can't win."

"You're wrong, Lieutenant. I've won just for having taken up the fight."

Matt digested the Indian's logic and could not help feeling increased respect for the renegade. "Perhaps you have, in your own way, but enough brave men have died on both sides in the interest of your goals. I have spoken with your father, Red Wing, and he too is angry with you for your violation of the treaty."

The mention of his father made Eagle Flies Alone grimace, even though he wished to show no expression. "My father is a fool, just like the other old squaws who have given our land away to the white man."

"No, he's not a fool," Matt said with a slight shake of his

head. "He is a wise man who knows the futility of making war against our numbers."

Eagle Flies Alone looked slowly to the right and then to the left, and his gaze swept across the plains. "Hear me, this land once belonged to the Arapaho. We have lived here in our own way, hunting and taking only what we needed. Now the white man has come, the buffalo are gone, and the land is being used to graze cattle." His eyes went to Ramsey's face and the hatred was obvious. "They are not our cattle. They belong to him and men like him. While his cattle grow fat on Arapaho grass, our people come to your agency to beg for corn and clothing. He is the one I would make war with, Lieutenant, not you."

Ramsey remained silent, but his eyes narrowed and his grip tightened on the stock of the Winchester lying at the ready across his lap. Kincaid glanced once at Ramsey and then back to Eagle Flies Alone.

"Mr. Ramsey did not write the treaty, nor did you or I. He has a legal document from Washington giving him the right to graze cattle on these plains. You have no legal right to stop him."

"I know nothing of your word 'legal,' but if what you call that word is supposed to be the same as what is right, then the word is no more just than the peace documents our fathers signed."

Deep in his heart, Kincaid had no choice but to sympathize, and even agree with, the Indian's viewpoint. But he had a mission to complete, and his personal feelings could have no bearing on the outcome of that mission.

"I am not here to discuss right or wrong with you. I am here to enforce the terms of the treaty and to offer you the chance to surrender and save the lives of your braves, who have fought honorably and well. Unless they wish to fight to the death, that is now over. You will surrender under my conditions or you will die."

Eagle Flies Alone watched Kincaid stoically, but a weariness seemed to have come over him and he asked softly, "What are the conditions you speak of?"

"Your unconditional surrender, your weapons turned in, and you personally standing trial for your crimes, as well as any others who have led in this insurrection."

"Others? There are no others. Eagle Flies Alone is the only

leader of fighting warriors left in the Arapaho nation. If there is guilt, no one is guilty but me."

"So be it. I trust you as a man of your word. If you surrender now, the others will be allowed to return to the reservation in return for their promise that they will live in peace and never take up weapons in violation of the treaty again. Is that agreed?"

There was pain on the warrior's face now, as though a dream had died within his heart, and he was silent for more than a minute. When he finally spoke there was strength in his voice and his eyes held steady on Kincaid's face. "I do not accept the terms of surrender."

"That's your choice," Matt said soberly. "You are the only one who can save the lives of the braves who have put their faith in you."

"I know that, Lieutenant. That is why I will offer you my own terms of surrender."

Kincaid's heartbeat quickened. "Your own terms? Let me hear them."

"I will fight one of you to the death. If I win, my braves and I will be allowed to ride north to Canada and live as we choose. If I lose, my braves will surrender under your terms. If you do not accept his, we will fight you now, here on the open plains."

Now it was Matt's turn to be silent as he thought about the counter-offer and the fact that the life of every man in the platoon was very likely at stake. Finally he nodded. "Very well, I accept your terms. You will fight me, and you name the weapons."

"No, Lieutenant," the Indian replied. "While I don't fear you, it's not you that I wish to fight. It is Ramsey. He is the man who takes our land, not you. If he wants it so badly, he should be willing to fight to the death to have it."

Ramsey's jaw was set, and his hard body stiffened in the saddle. "That's fine with me, Lieutenant," Ramsey said without breaking eye contact with Eagle Flies Alone. "Let him choose the weapons."

"Are you sure, Ramsey?"

"Never been so sure. Go ahead, Eagle Flies Alone. Your choice."

"Knives."

Ramsey nodded. "I thought so, and that's fine. I'll use my bare hands."

Even the Indian could not control the look of surprise that flashed across his face, and Windy joined Kincaid in a quizzical, almost unbelieving stare at the rancher.

"Did I hear what I think I heard, Matt?" the scout asked.

"I'm not sure. Did we, Ramsey?"

"You did. And we fight to the death."

A triumphant sneer curled across the Indian's lips. "You are a greater fool than I thought you were," he said, turning his mount away. "I will explain the terms of our agreement to my braves and they will abide by my decision."

Kincaid watched Eagle Flies Alone return to the line of warriors before his head snapped toward the rancher. "Are you crazy, Ramsey?"

Ramsey shrugged. "Probably. It's been said before."

"I can't let you fight him barehanded," Kincaid insisted. "There's no doubt that he's an expert with a knife."

"You can't? Doesn't look to me like you've got a hell of a lot of choice, Kincaid." Ramsey winked as he stepped from his saddle. "Back out on this, and you've broken your word with the featherheads. We can't have that, now can we?"

Neither of them was more than twenty-four years old, each stripped to the waist. One was bronzed by nature, the other through hours of toil in the sun. They were lean, sinewy men, and their bodies had not yet begun to succumb to the softness that comes with age and lassitude. Eagle Flies Alone held a long-bladed knife in his right hand, which he worked with a clenching movement of his fist. His tanned-leather leggings clung tightly to his thighs and the moccasins on his feet were silent in the grass. He watched curiously as his opponent prepared for battle.

"Matt, I think our boy there's suffered a complete misfire," Windy said as Ramsey stooped and pulled the boots from his feet and tossed them aside. "Too long in the sun, I'd say."

There was a grim look on Ramsey's face as he straightened, but he smiled tightly and looked up at Windy. "Hide and watch, oldtimer. You might learn something."

Completely baffled, Kincaid shrugged and made no response as Ramsey stepped forward to move cautiously around Eagle Flies Alone in a half-circle. With his fingers extended and pressed together, he rotated his hands in a testing motion and watched the Indian. "All right," he said in a distant voice, as if he were living in another time, "I'm ready when you are."

The warrior crouched in a wide-legged stance, his body bent slightly at the waist and arms held wide, the gleaming blade carving menacing arcs before him. The two men moved warily in a clockwise circle. Then Eagle Flies Alone lunged forward and the knife sliced downward, but Ramsey skipped away unscathed. The Indian recovered quickly and brought his knife back to a defensive position in front of his chest before striking out again. This time the razor-sharp blade slashed across the white man's forearm.

Eagle Flies Alone grinned as blood spurted forth and made a red trail down Ramsey's arm. The rancher seemed not to have noticed. He might well have been in a trance, so rigid was his fixed gaze on the Indian's face. Kincaid and Windy shared a worried glance before looking back to the two combatants.

Eagle Flies Alone watched, impassive once again, and waited for another opening. And when he lunged forward a third time, Ramsey's hand lashed out like a striking snake and the calloused heel of his palm smashed against the Indian's forearm. Eagle Flies Alone winced in pain, but Ramsey didn't pursue, choosing instead to continue his constant circling, his hands moving in the air like pistons on a steam engine. The warrior switched the knife to his left hand and shook his right arm to ward off the numbness. Ramsey struck again with catlike speed, and the edge of his hand slammed against Eagle Flies Alone's right forearm again. The brave's hand dropped to his side, and it was obvious the bone had been broken. Eagle Flies Alone slashed desperately with the knife and barely nicked Ramsey's left shoulder, but the rancher moved away, totally oblivious to the blood running down his back. His eyes were glazed over and there was no apparent indication of pain.

The Indian was hurting badly and his forearm began to swell midway to the elbow. He crouched even lower as he watched Ramsey's hands and waited. But it was not the rancher's hands that were a threat to him this time. With a sudden twist of his body, his bare left foot shot out and his heel caught his opponent squarely in the chest and sent him stumbling backward before the Indian could react with a feeble thrust of the knife. Again, Ramsey didn't press the attack.

When the warrior recovered there was a desperate look in his eyes, the look of a man who was beaten but would not give up. He lunged wildly at Ramsey again with an awkward jab of the knife, and when the blade passed by harmlessly, Ramsey kicked again with a scream that came from deep in his guts, and the heel of his foot smacked against the other man's jaw and sent the Indian in a spinning, tumbling sprawl to the ground. Ramsey did not close on the fallen man, choosing instead to continue his circling.

Dazed, Eagle Flies Alone staggered to his feet and picked up the knife from where it had fallen. Ramsey nodded his approval and stalked his prey once more. The Indian was nearly defenseless now, but if he could be faulted for anything, it certainly wasn't lack of courage. He lashed out with the knife in a series of lunges that were ineffective and poorly timed. Ramsey appeared to be looking *through* his man, not *at* him, and continued to circle as he jumped away from the blade. With the Indian's last thrust, the rancher's right hand smashed across his opponent's left forearm and the knife dropped noiselessly to the grass.

There was a startled look on the Indian's face as he backed away and struggled to bring his left hand up to defend his head, but the hand would not rise and dangled limply on a second broken arm. It was then that Ramsey attacked, first with a chopping left to the neck, and then slamming the heel of his right palm against the warrior's nose.

A stunned look filled the young brave's eyes as he staggered once, then lost his footing and fell backward on the grass, dead before he hit the ground. His body twitched once before he lay still in the matted grass, his once prominent nose smashed flat against his face.

Ramsey watched his fallen opponent silently, still crouched over with hands poised to strike, until the blankness melted from his eyes. He glanced around once as if orienting himself, looked one more time at the dead man lying at his feet, then turned away. Without saying a word, he pulled his socks and boots back on and slipped his arms into his shirt and began tucking the material in at his waist.

"Never seen anything like it," Windy said, not trying to conceal the awe in his voice.

"Neither have I," Matt concurred. "What killed him?"

"His nose bone is driven into his brain," Ramsey said offhandedly as he stomped into his boots. "I learned a few things like that in Singapore when I was in with the merchant fleet."

Kincaid said, continuing to stare at the dead Indian, "He was out of it anyway. Did you have to kill him?"

Ramsey looked up with something nearing impatience in his eyes. "It was a fight to the death, wasn't it? He called it, I didn't. Besides, it would have been a dishonor to shame him by sparing his life. You would've hung him anyway. He was a fighter and deserved better than that."

Matt nodded. "Yeah, I suppose we would have. Damn, that was scary."

"There is only one purpose for this method of fighting, Lieutenant," Ramsey said as he swung into his saddle, "and that is to kill. Remember that the next time you make love to somebody's sister."

"Go on back to the ranks, Ramsey. Have Sergeant Olsen get out the medicine kit and wrap your arm and put a bandage on that shoulder wound." Kincaid said, turning in the saddle and ignoring Ramsey's threat. "Lieutenant Davis!"

Davis pulled up beside Kincaid. "Yessir?"

"Have a detail collect the weapons from those braves, then escort them back to the agency." Kincaid looked at the silent warriors who had not moved nor spoken during or after the fight, then turned to Wingfoot. "Your chief is dead. He gave his word to me that if he lost the fight, you and his other followers would surrender peacefully. Do you intend to uphold his honor and accept the terms of our agreement?"

Wingfoot's eyes slowly left the fallen warrior's body and drifted to Kincaid's face. "We do," he said softly.

"Good. You too are a man of honor. Have your chief's body loaded on his horse and your people can bury him however they wish. We will be going back to the agency now."

Wingfoot hesitated before saying, "One more thing. There is an old man bound and gagged at our camp beside the bluff. His name is Gray Bear and he will die if he's not released."

"Thank you, Wingfoot. I'll see that he is taken care of."

Wingfoot nodded, handed his rifle and knife to Lieutenant Davis, then turned his horse and rode slowly toward those waiting in the distance.

It was a cool morning, and dark clouds scudded across the horizon. A chill wind blew on the agency street in shifting gusts, and dust devils raced away in twisting funnels to dissipate and die on the grassland. Four old Indians waited on the street, impervious to the weather and sitting their ponies with a sort of forlorn pride.

Kincaid approached them on foot and the driving dust lashed against his back as he stopped and looked up. "Thank you for your help, Red Wing. Do I have your personal word that those involved in your son's insurrection will be properly punished in accordance with Arapaho law?"

There was no mistaking the look of grief on the old warrior's face. "You have, Lieutenant. I am sorry for what my son did. He would have been a great chieftan in another time."

"Yes, he would have. In another time," Matt replied with sincerity before turning to the ancient medicine man. "How are you feeling, Gray Bear?"

"My heart is heavy," the old man replied in a faltering voice. "I did not wish to see war between our two peoples again in my lifetime. We have lost the struggle and now must accept our fate."

A heavy sadness crept into Kincaid's heart, which he wished to ignore but couldn't. "I would like to see the consequences of that fate be less than they are. There has been much needless death for your people as well as for mine. Go now, and live in peace."

The four raised their hands, palms outward, then turned and rode away with the following wind shifting the feathers wildly in their hair and curling their ponies' tails around their haunches. A feeling of desolation came over Kincaid as he watched them move onto the plains, four old men who had no choice but to continue to lead. He turned and walked quickly to where six mounted riders waited with collars folded up around their necks and hatbrims bending on the strong wind.

Kincaid stopped by Ramsey's horse and looked up, shielding his eyes from the dust with a hand. "Ramsey, I know we have a difference of opinion about one thing, but that's something neither of us can do anything about. I'd like to thank you for your help in this crisis," Matt said, taking the hand from his face and offering it in friendship.

Ramsey looked down at the hand for long moments before leaning over and grasping it firmly. "My pleasure, Lieutenant. Any time." He hesitated. "We'll try to do a little better job of keeping our cattle on our side of the line from now on."

"I'd appreciate that. Can I ask one more favor?"

"You can ask."

"Give my best regards to Betty Jo?"

Ramsey paused again and the two men stared at each other until a hesitant grin touched the young rancher's lips. "Sure, Lieutenant. Be glad to. I'm sure she'll appreciate the thought. Stop by and see us next time you're up this way."

"Thanks, I'll do that. Why not? You've got the best damned drinkin' whiskey in the territory."

Ramsey's cautious grin melted into a smile. "Sure do. And a sister to match. Take care," he said, touching spurs to his horse's flanks, and the cattlemen rode down the street in the opposite direction from which the Arapaho had gone.

The platoon was mounted along the street, awaiting orders from their commanding officer, who moved toward them now, but paused when he saw Doug Collins standing in front of the agency.

"See you next time around, Doug," Kincaid called over the whistling of the wind. "Keep up those double rations until you hear otherwise. I'll be sending a work detail back here in a week or so to help with the rebuilding of the compound."

"Will do, Matt. Thanks for everything," Collins replied before scurrying inside and out of the chill.

Kincaid waved and moved along the mounted riders until he found Private Pappas, his heavily bandaged leg splinted against movement and hanging down free of the stirrup. "You going to be able to ride, Ike?"

"We're going home, sir," Pappas replied with a weak smile. "I'll make it."

"I'm sure you will. Just hang in there and we'll have you back to your lady before you know it."

"I hope so, sir. For whatever good it's going to do."

Kincaid patted the soldier's thigh as he moved away. "She'll be there, Ike. Believe it, she'll be there."

His foot found the stirrup and Kincaid swung onto his horse, and he and Windy led the company down the street. The first raindrops splattered across their faces and into the dust of the street, leaving dark red craters in the dull brown dirt.

Mandalian looked at the sky and knew they were in for a heavy storm. "Guess the old bastard was right, huh, Matt?"

"What do you mean, Windy?"

"Old Gray Bear and that damned prediction of his that brought us here in the first place. Looks like there's gonna be green arrows as far as the eye can see."

"Yeah, guess he was, at that," Kincaid replied, looking upward at the falling rain, which washed across his face. But his mind was on another person. Beautiful and warm and soft. And he knew he would never see her again.

fourteen

Captain Warner Conway sat behind his desk with the paybook at one elbow and a stack of bills beside the other. He pressed his fingertips together and looked up at the huge private standing at attention before him.

"This seems to be where all the trouble starts, doesn't it, Private?" he asked in an authoritative but not demanding voice.

"Pardon me, sir?" Malone asked.

"Payday. When you get paid you go berserk and inevitably wind up on Sergeant Cohen's shitlist."

"Never happen again, sir. You have me bleedin' word on that," Malone said earnestly.

Conway sighed and counted thirteen dollars from the stack, shoved the money toward Malone, and turned the paybook for his signature. "That word you're so proud of, Private, seems to be a highly flexible contract. From now on, if—"

Sergeant Cohen poked his head around the doorjamb. "Sorry to interrupt you, sir, but the guard on the west wall just reported. First Platoon's comin' in and lookin' bad. Johnson said he could make out at least six empty saddles."

Captain Conway was out from behind his desk and on the way to the door before Cohen could finish speaking. "Keep an eye on that payroll, Sarge," he said over his shoulder as he stepped from the building and pulled his hat on his head. "I'll be back in a little while."

His step faltered as he passed by his quarters, and he glanced once toward the window. He could see his wife and Sarah Williams seated at the kitchen table and talking amicably while sharing morning tea. The girl had made her decision to leave Pappas if he reenlisted, and she had been upset and had come to Flora for moral support. The mention of the empty saddles flashed through Conway's mind and he hoped the girl hadn't made a weak decision that she would regret for the rest of her life. Then his jaw tightened and he moved toward the main gate again with crisp, military strides.

It was obvious that both men and mounts of First Platoon were nearing exhaustion as they rode wearily into the outpost. When the troops dismounted, Kincaid called them to attention, and even the wounded soldiers stiffly pulled themselves to an erect posture. While he returned Kincaid's salute, Conway's eyes swept down the line and he saw Pappas standing there with his right leg held rigidly in its splint. The captain exhaled what might have been a sigh of relief and his gaze returned to Lieutenant Kincaid.

"Looks like you've had a rough patrol, Lieutenant."

"We did, sir. Eight dead, four wounded, and two mounts lost. We accomplished our mission and the uprising has been put down."

"I'm very sorry to hear about your casualties, Lieutenant. After you've had a chance to rest, I'll need a full, handwritten report. Also, I'll want a detailed oral description from you delineating exactly what happened."

"Certainly, sir. I can give that to you now, if you'd like."

"There's no hurry. Get some rest first. Lieutenant Davis?"

"Yessir?" Davis said, stepping forward smartly.

"I have some good news for one of your men. Walk with me to congratulate him."

"Be glad to, sir," Davis replied, moving in step with Conway.

As they walked down the line, Conway glanced once toward his quarters and saw Flora and the girl standing beneath the awning. Sarah Williams had her hands clutched to her face, and from the throbbing of her shoulders he knew she was crying.

They stopped before Ike Pappas, and the soldier tried to pull himself to a more correct position of attention.

"At ease, soldier. You look like you've been through hell," Conway said. "Relax and we'll get you medical aid as quickly as possible." A smile spread across the captain's face. "But I wanted to be the first to congratulate you. Welcome back, Corporal Pappas."

There was a bewildered look in Pappas' eyes as he asked, "Beg pardon, sir?"

"Your promotion came through. Easy Company could use another good squad leader."

Pappas' eyes drifted to the young woman in the yellow dress who was watching him from across the parade, then his gaze snapped back to hold unwaveringly on the captain's face. His lips were stretched tight in grim determination.

"Thank you, sir," Pappas said, snapping a salute. "I'll do my best, sir."

Conway watched him closely. "I don't wish to influence your decision about reenlisting, Corporal. Does that mean you intend to remain in the service?"

"That's what it means, sir."

Conway returned the salute, as did Davis, then both officers shook the new noncom's hand.

"Lieutenant Davis," Conway said with a quick sideways glance, "there is someone special waiting to see the corporal. Dismiss him and then dismiss the rest of the company. When their horses have been cared for, make sure they get a good hot meal. After they've rested, issue a two-day pass to each of them. Their pay is waiting for them in my office."

"Yessir. Corporal Pappas, you're dismissed."

Pappas saluted again, then hobbled slowly toward the woman who continued to stare at him as though frozen in place. He stopped halfway between the ranks and the officers' quarters and waited for her to come to him. The girl hesitated a moment longer, then ran toward him with skirts flying and tears streaming down her face. Her arms went around him and she kissed him wildly and tried to talk at the same time.

"Ike . . . I love you, Ike . . . I love you . . . you're hurt . . . I love you, darling . . . please don't leave me again . . . I . . ."

Pappas' arms closed around her and he pulled her to him in a crushing embrace. "Slow down, honey. Slow down. I'm all right. I'll be as good as new in a few days." He grasped her shoulders gently and pushed her away to look into her eyes. "And I'll be able to take over my new duties," he said slowly. "I'm a squad leader now. I've been promoted to lance corporal."

"You . . . what?"

"I've been promoted, Sarah. I'm going to stay in the service."

She looked up at him and tried to blink the tears away from her long lashes, but they continued to flow down her cheeks.

Pappas gently brushed a droplet away with his thumb. "I'm sorry, honey. The others are counting on me. I can't let them down."

Salty tears ran into the corners of her trembling mouth and she tried to speak, but the words wouldn't come. And when they finally did, she said in a quivering voice, "I love you, Ike Pappas. I don't care what you do or who you are. I love you and I want to be with you. I want to be your wife."

Pappas slowly pulled her to his chest and his arms went around her again. He pressed his face gently to hers, and twin tears trickled down his cheeks. "I love you too, Mrs. Pappas," he said as he rocked her in his arms.

Behind them the words, "Platoooon, dissssmissssed!" rolled across the parade and the men of Easy Company moved away. Even though weary, exhausted and hurt, they walked with dignity, and pride was written on their faces. After a short pass and a little fun in town, they would be back on combat patrol again. They knew not who would be the next man to fall, but they did know that, whomever he was, he would not die without honor.

SPECIAL PREVIEW

Here are the opening scenes
from

EASY COMPANY AND THE WHITE MAN'S PATH

the next novel in Jove's exciting
new High Plains adventure series

EASY COMPANY

Coming next month!

"While visiting an Indian village in one of the Dakotas, many years ago, I rode up to the head chief's lodge, where I expected to remain for the night. The chief came out and received me, while, at the same time, his squaw unsaddled my horse and placed the equipment alongside their teepee. I asked the chief if they would be safe there, whereupon he observed, 'Yes, there isn't a white man within two days' ride of here.'"

—from *The Frontier Trail,*
by Homer W. Wheeler; quotation attributed to Bishop Whipple

one

An uneasy quiet lay over Outpost Number Nine. Mr. Lo was behaving himself for the time being, but a yearning for peace did not seem to run very deep in the Indians of 1877. And as far west as the Wyoming Territory, where Outpost Number Nine was located, it hardly extended below the surface.

Such were the sentiments of Easy Company's first sergeant, Ben Cohen, a longtime veteran of the Indian Wars. Easy Company was a contingent of mounted infantry, sometimes called 'dragoons' by the public and press, but that was a generic term loosely applied to damn near any soldier that rode a horse, and it was therefore not a very accurate designation. Either way, Easy had to be ready to mount up at a split second's notice and ride off to restore order. Thus it behooved (a favorite Cohen word) a good top kick to keep his men on their toes. Cohen did this by keeping them so busy—regrading roads, stringing telegraph wire, repairing fortifications, scrubbing and polishing everything that didn't move, collecting and laying in about twenty years' supply of wood, toting "honey buckets"—that riding into battle would come as welcome relief.

Cohen came out of the orderly room and stood looking over the parade, automatically scanning the outpost, *his* outpost, as if a wall might have fallen down since morning assembly. One hadn't, nor was it likely to, unless the Indians acquired artillery.

The parade was empty, save for a crew digging a new latrine pit near the enlisted barracks. Poor beggars'd be taking the sun full now. Cohen glanced at the sun. It was getting on toward noon of an early-summer day. Beginning to feel the heat, Cohen strode off toward the distant pit detail.

The detail had been drawn from Mr. Allison's Third Platoon. Cohen could see the broad, bare, heaving shoulders of Private Jeremy Enright, formerly James Evinrude. Getting closer, he distinguished the bullet-headed Private Moor, the new recruit Private Barrett, the loudmouthed, brawling Private Popper, and another new recruit named John Gillies, an undersized runt from the New York slums, whom the men disparagingly called Weasel. That was five. Cohen thought he'd detailed six. Then he saw Private Kazmaier, a man of low intelligence but high cunning, emerge from the mess toting a bucket of water. Cohen guessed it had probably taken Kazmaier a half-hour to get the water.

"How's it going?" Cohen asked, letting them know he hadn't forgotten about them.

"Real peachy, Sarge."

Cohen eyed Moore. Silly remarks were his trademark. "Be sure to make it deep enough. But stop when you hit water."

"How far down's the water table?" asked Enright, an ex-farmer who was curious about such things.

"You'll find out." Cohen watched Kazmaier gently set the bucket down. "Why don't you men take a break, refresh yourselves. Let Kazmaier dig for a while."

They scrambled out and Kazmaier promptly leapt in, where he dug with unusual zest until Cohen was safely back in the orderly room.

Letting his spade drop, Kazmaier complained, "Hell, you'd think we was niggers, the way he makes us go in this sun." His pale blue eyes glared from his nut-brown face.

"You *do* look kinda dark, Kaz. Gittin' darker, too," Moore observed.

"Yeah, but at least *I* started out *white*. *Barrett's* the one that's got a lot of explainin' to do."

Barrett eyed Kazmaier narrowly. Barrett was tall, well built, and reasonably good looking. But his skin was naturally darker than most, his hair thick and black, his cheekbones high and angled, his nostrils very slightly flared, and his lips thicker and browner than most. He did appear to be, in Kazmaier's favorite phrase, a "mongrelized bastard".

Barrett's eyes were mere slits now. "I told you bastards, I got Injun blood way back somewhere. Hell, I *hate* niggers."

Kazmaier, undaunted, smiled nastily. "An' Weasel too . . ."

"Goddammit!" squawked the narrow-featured Gillies, "I'm Armenian, an' Turk besides."

Barrett wished he'd thought of that.

"'Cept Weasel's such a runt," continued Kazmaier. "I never seen a nigger runt."

"An' I never seed a blue-eyed asshole," cried Gillies, reaching for a spade handle.

"Whaddaya think they do down South?" interjected Moore, trying to smooth things over.

"Whaddaya mean?" demanded Kazmaier.

"I mean the army. They're supposed to be all niggers down there. Who do you reckon digs *their* latrines—Injuns?"

"The officers too?"

"Too? Too what?"

"They niggers too?"

"Naw. *They're* white."

"Bet they're downright ecstatic about *that* command."

"But it's not just because of the coloreds," said Enright, joining the discussion as he climbed back down into the pit, "who ain't supposed to be all that bad as fighters. Naw, it's something more than that." He started digging. "This handgun we got, the Scoff? There ain't all that many of them around, and I hear we only got them because the army got a bargain. Or that's what they say. But it's a good gun. Smith & Wesson makes good guns. And the *real* reason it ain't admired is that the designer, Schofield, was once an officer with the Tenth Cav—that's one of the colored outfits—and the big brass don't think much of them officers, don't like to single 'em out for any kind of notice."

"How come? Schofield prob'ly didn't have no choice who he commanded. Army'll screw you, give 'em half a chance."

"Maybe so, but there's some that think an officer should resign his commission 'fore taking a command like that. Like a white officer shouldn't have to command coloreds."

"Someone's gotta," said Moore.

"What for?" demanded Kazmaier. "Let them bastards pick cotton, that's all they're good for."

"Like I said, the Ninth and Tenth ain't supposed to be bad," observed Enright mildly. "And I hear tell a lot of cowboys are colored."

"So what? So're some Injuns. An' a lot of them greasy brown bastards from down Mexicali way. That don't make it *right*." Kazmaier found himself in rare possession of a principle. "Anyway, how do you know all that stuff about Schofield and the niggers?"

"Lieutenant Kincaid," replied Enright.

"Oh, yeah? You and him is buddies, that it?" Kazmaier asked.

"Nope," said Enright, heaving a load of dirt at Kazmaier.

"*I* would've," said Barrett.

"You would've what?" asked Popper.

"Resigned my commission. I've had somethin' to do with niggers in my time—"

"I'll bet you have," sneered Kazmaier.

"—An' there ain't nothin' lower. The only thing worse'n an Injun is a nigger." He seemed excessively worked up, his neck corded, eyes roving wildly. "If'n I was down South watchin' that Tenth Cav go up against Mr. Lo, I wouldn't hardly know who to root for. Hellfire, it'd sure be tough to choose."

"Yeah," said Popper, matching Kazmaier's sneer and measuring Barrett. Popper liked to fight, to brawl, it was about all he knew. He didn't always win, but he always came back for more. Barrett was a new man, a big man, and thus far untested. Popper couldn't resist. "*I've* met a few coloreds in my day and I don't think much of them either, but they're better'n some—"

"They're *all* scum," insisted Barrett.

"—They're one hell of a lot better'n some what won't admit they're niggers, what call themselves 'part Injun.' How's *that* for bein' colored—colored *yella*!"

Barrett thought it over, thinking about what Popper meant, thinking the other men knew what he meant, maybe even agreed, even Enright. "Get up, Popper," he growled.

"I don't git up fer no nigger *or* no Injun."

"Then take it settin' down," said Barrett, and strode towards him.

Popper was on his feet in a flash, but not fast enough to avoid a hard left. He staggered backwards, shaking it off. The bastard's a lefty, he thought, that's his good hand.

It wasn't. Barrett feinted another left hook, but then lifted Popper clear off the ground with a right, dug up into his belly.

Sergeant Cohen had heard the clamor and came barreling out of the orderly room. The first sergeant, the company's undisputed Top Fist, loved a good fight.

Getting near, though, he saw that this one wasn't so good. The big recruit, Barrett, was making mincemeat out of Popper, filling Popper's big, loud mouth with knuckles. And doing it fast. Cohen would have preferred a longer, more drawn-out engagement.

Cohen exchanged glances with Private Enright, another man who fought little because he fought so well. Just the week before, in town, Cohen had watched Enright do a bullwhacker the way Barrett was doing Popper.

Popper suddenly shot backwards and pitched into the pit, where Enright caught him. Enright got a good hold on Popper and heaved him back out, where the man lay unconscious in the dust.

"Moore, Kazmaier, Gillies," said Cohen, "haul Popper back to the barracks." He shook his head. "He better start saving his fighting for Mr. Lo. As for you, Barrett, I don't know how this started, but Popper—"

"Popper started it, Sarge," said Gillies.

"Popper's a nigger-lover," added Barrett.

Cohen gave Barrett a look, then said, "That ain't necessary."

"The big guy really tore up Popper's ass, didn't he?" said a young, nasal voice.

They all looked to where a boy stood. Fifteen, sixteen years old, he was small, but not much smaller than Gillies, upon whom he'd fastened his eyes. "You're Weasel, aintcha?"

"Who the hell let you in *this* time, Billy?" demanded Cohen.

"Who's he, Sarge?" snarled Gillies. "Dependent kid?"

"This kid? Hell, no, look at him, scrawnier than hell and near dressed in rags. He's from a town near fifty miles from here. Scares up a pony, rides it over, bothers the bejesus out of us. Wants to be an effin' soldier. All he *is*, though, is a pain in the ass. C'mon, now, Billy, beat it. Or go over and beg somethin' at the sutler's. An' the rest of you get this clown Popper inside before he roasts to death."

They dragged poor Popper into the barracks with Billy right behind, as if Cohen had never spoken to him. As they all disappeared into the barracks, Weasel could be heard yelling, "For Chrissakes, kid, beat it!"

"Kid's a real pest," said Cohen. "Always around, but as far as I can tell he don't have shit for a family, so . . ."

Enright figured that hardly anyone out there at Outpost Nine, in the middle of Wyoming, had "shit for a family." If they had, they probably wouldn't be there.

"You two finish this hole, it's near done anyway," said Cohen. "I got plans for those other fellers. They're gonna wish . . ." But he turned and walked off without finishing his threat.

"How come he's sore at them?" wondered Barrett.

Enright was silent.

"Huh?" prompted Barrett.

"He just gets sore sometimes, that's all. He's the first sergeant, he's allowed."

"Don't seem fair."

Enright's head was down and he kept it down.

"I said it don't seem fair," Barrett repeated.

"Oh, he's fair about anything important. Now, are you gonna dig or think about what a great fighter you are?"

"I looked good, huh?" but there was no response.

Barrett dug. They both dug. Barrett kept making friendly overtures to Enright and kept being ignored. A look of hurt began to come over his face.

They soon had the hole completed and they climbed out.

"Enright? What's wrong?" Hell, a man could live alone, draw upon his own resources, and do all right if he had to, but not in the army. You had to have at least *one* buddy. "I wanna be friends," Barrett almost whined.

"I'm not sure I want to be friends with you," muttered Enright.

"But . . . but why?"

Enright looked at him, then reached out and started poking his chest with his finger for emphasis as he said, "Because I think you were wrong back there. Wrong *then*, and wrong, *period*."

"About *what*?"

"About coloreds," said Enright simply, mopping his brow and pushing his graying hair back. Enright was in his thirties, overage for a private. He'd fought in the War, mustered out, gone home to Maine, and then watched his family and all its branches wither and die. The last one, his son, had been killed in a fight and Enright had killed the killer. Then he'd rejoined the army. The law had come after him, found him, but then decided they didn't want him after all. They'd told him to change his name and let him stay on at Outpost Nine. He'd changed it, to Jeremy Enright, and didn't mind the change. He figured many of the men out there had something to hide and weren't using the names they were born with.

"I've seen a lot more than you have, Barrett, of life, of war . . . of *men*. I've known a number of coloreds, fought alongside some, and there were a few I wouldn't mind sidin' to hell and back, proud to call 'em my friend."

Barrett was watching Enright steadily, closely.

"And I've never seen a colored," continued Enright, "till I was over twenty, so it's not like I was raised with 'em. There are good ones and bad ones, just like anyone, and you're a fool to think the way you do."

Enright was one of the few men that Barrett held in high regard. Sure, he admired Matt Kincaid and Captain Conway—and even Sergeant Cohen—but the men he was placing Enright among were the men he lived with, slept with, ate with, pissed alongside, the mostly dirty but mainly stupid enlisted men.

He reached out and touched Enright, who almost pulled away but didn't. Barrett's face softened, and a strange look came into his eyes.

"I was born on the twenty-sixth of April," said Barrett slowly, in a monotone, "in Fredericksburg, Virginia. That was the first time. There were thirteen children in my family, seven sons and six daughters. I was the third oldest. Had me an older sister and an older brother. The *second* time I was born, I was twelve years old, it was in 1866. And I've studied the language, I can speak it, I can talk with the Absaroka. . . ."

Enright listened closely, partly out of courtesy but also because it sounded so strange. Not just the words but the delivery. Had the sun gotten to the tall, black-haired man? His eyes certainly had a fevered look. Maybe Popper'd gotten a blow in that no one had seen. . . .

Absaroka. Where had he heard that before?

"Does that mean anything to you?" asked Barrett, his eyes slowly focusing on Enright.

"Other than that you're twenty-three years old, no."

This time Barrett looked like he was working up a full head of steam. He opened his mouth . . . but then the two of them saw a strange thing approaching. Actually it wasn't all that strange, just the large, portable, wooden latrine that was headed their way, carried by six grinning privates. What was so funny about carrying a latrine?

"The hole's finished, ain't it?" asked one of the porters, and Enright nodded. "Don't fall in," he said pleasantly, "or we'll have to toss you a rope."

"Haw-haw-haw," intoned another porter.

They placed the latrine snugly down over the hole and then, without a word, marched off. They went as far as the barracks but didn't enter; instead they hung around out front, keeping a sly watch on the latrine.

Enright saw them there, and wondered what was going on. But Barrett took no similar notice. He'd gotten that look back in his eyes. He was far away.

Enright studied him for a long while, then finally asked, "You all right?"

Barrett snapped out of it, blinking and shaking his head. "Yeah, I'm fine. But . . ." He took a deep breath. "But what you said before . . ." He was giving something one hell of a lot of thought. "Look, there's something no one knows, *no one*, and I probably shouldn't tell you, but I trust you. You're not like the rest. You're older, you're sensible an' you've got to understand that when I was talking about"—his lips compressed—"about niggers before, sounding the way I did, it's . . . it's because I'm one-quarter colored myself."

"What!?"

"Shhhhh!" Barrett's eyes practically popped from his head.

Enright blinked and sagged against the latrine.

"I guess that makes me a mulatto," Barrett concluded.

"Jeez," oozed Enright, "I guess so. You do mean *colored* colored."

Barrett nodded. "Or maybe I'm a quadroon."

Enright thought that was a dance they did down around New Orleans. "But why, Barrett? How come you're tryin' to be white?"

"You know why. The way I talked before is the way most white men talk about colored folk. I couldn't take it. Not without having to fight. An' how do you think I'd look, riding with the Tenth Cav?"

"Well, hell, I don't see what you're so goddamned worked up about. You *look* white enough to me, 'spite of what that asshole Kazmaier says."

"But that's the thing. I'm not. It's a lie. And it's tearing me apart. Now, I've heard talk of how hard it is for the Indian to follow the white man's path. And I've also read where a white man can become an Indian but an Indian can't become a white man."

"What's that supposed to mean?"

"Dunno, exactly. You figure it out. Can't civilize an Injun, maybe. But I've got the same problem. I've chosen the white man's path—"

"Sure have," commented Enright, recalling the earlier racial outbursts.

"—But it's not easy. I'm not sure I can do it. Maybe I need help." He looked hard at Enright. "And then there's something else, a calling I have. I hear voices. . . ."

"What?" Enright looked around. He didn't hear anyone.

"In my head. I hear them in my head."

"What do they say?"

Barrett only smiled.

"Like that stuff before, the twenty-sixth of April and Fredericksburg and stuff like that?" Enright said.

Barrett stared at him, slightly astonished. "*You* hear the same voices too?"

"No, dammit. That's what *you* said, just before."

"*I* didn't say anything," said Barrett soothingly, as if to imply that Enright was mad and had to be treated gently. Then Barrett got that faraway look again.

Here it comes, thought Enright. "Look, Jeff—that's your name, isn't it? Jeff?—let's head for the mess and see if Dutch has got some fresh coffee."

"Black soup."

"What?" But Barrett said no more. Damn. Probably some special colored saying. Enright hung his head. How come

Barrett had to tell *him* all that stuff?

The two men walked off toward the mess.

The men outside the barracks watched them go, their faces, for some reason, glum with disappointment. Then they watched little Billy harass Weasel Gillies, following him in and out of the barracks.

"Them two deserve each other. Which one's worse, do you figger?"

"Kid's probably a thief."

"And Weasel ain't? He'd steal his mother's crutch."

"How do you know?"

"I know them kind. I been to the cities, I know what kind of scum grows up there."

"Don't grow very tall, it seems."

As they laughed about that, the door to the latrine slowly swung open. And then an Indian face appeared, or a face grotesquely smeared with garish pigment to resemble that of a bloodthirsty brave hot on the warpath—a presence of dubious comfort, if not outright shock, to anyone seeking relief inside the latrine.

The "warrior" looked about, determined that Enright and Barrett were gone, and then leaped from the latrine. The paint on his face masked any expression, but as he hustled toward the barracks he began squawking like crazy.